SERPENT'S TOOTH

Eric Johansson lives in Fox Creek with his elderly grandmother. But young Carver Ellis discovers him dead in his bed, having been severely beaten. Then, unfortunately for Ellis, the police officer arrives on the scene already convinced that Ellis murdered the victim. Victoria Sears, and her friend down-mountain, Lynn Hanson, work with Deputy Richard Wroten to clear Ellis and uncover why Johansson died. Can they do it before a crucial piece of evidence disappears?

Books by Michael R. Collings
in the Linford Mystery Library:

DEVIL'S PLAGUE

MICHAEL R. COLLINGS

SERPENT'S TOOTH

Complete and Unabridged

LINFORD
Leicester

First published in Great Britain

First Linford Edition
published 2012

British Library CIP Data

Collings, Michael R.
   Serpent's tooth.- -(Linford mystery library)
   1. Detective and mystery stories.
   2. Large type books.
   I. Title II. Series
   813.6–dc23

   ISBN 978–1–4448–1328–9

Published by
F. A. Thorpe (Publishing)
Anstey, Leicestershire

Set by Words & Graphics Ltd.
Anstey, Leicestershire
Printed and bound in Great Britain by
T. J. International Ltd., Padstow, Cornwall

This book is printed on acid-free paper

Dedication

For Judi,
with gratitude for her initial request so
many years ago that I write a mystery
and
For Robert Reginald,
with thanks for words of advice
whispered into my artificial ears

'How sharper than a serpent's tooth it is
To have a thankless child!'

— William Shakespeare,
King Lear, Act I, Scene IV.

Prologue

The late afternoon sun blazed down on the narrow rutted road that ran behind the field, baking the already red-tinted earth to the consistency of brick.

For many smaller creatures, the direct sun was the mortal enemy. It was too hot. It was too sharp. It was too bright. It robbed them of the comforting brindled patterns of light and shadow that so often offered them protection. For some, it marked the time when predators might lurk in damp grasses, on warm rocks, in the cloudless skies, circling and watching and waiting for a single, fatal momentary lapse . . . for the chance to kill.

For the serpent, however, the warmth felt . . . well, it felt right. Life-giving. Bracing. It lay stretched across the two-lane track, completely motionless. It looked more like a thick, gnarled stick — perhaps three feet long — tossed negligently to one side by an unwary passerby than like the venom-filled stalker that it was.

It had not moved for long minutes now.

It might almost have been dead, except for the occasional flicker of a black, forked tongue as it tasted the still, pungent air.

At this time of the year, with the first harvest just underway, no one used the back road very much. Oh, one of the local farmers might trundle along in a tractor now and again, preferring to take the shorter but rougher route rather than the smoothly surfaced county highway on the far side of the field.

Or a couple of boys on furlough from the tedium of daily chores might tramp that way on their trek to the not-too-distant river and a favorite swimming hole, where they could enjoy some innocent horseplay far from parents' prying eyes.

But on the whole, like today, the road belonged to the snake. The only other signs of life were situated clear across the field, where a small crew was combining thigh-high wheat in long, straight rows.

Another group would follow with the baler, scooping up the discarded straw and binding it in smallish rectangular bales. A third group would finish the job, hoisting the bales manually onto a noisome flat-bed truck, where the last two or three hands would stack them for transport to back to the farm.

There were more modern machines that could do all of these disparate tasks without relying on human muscle-power, of course, but this was a small field, one of only four belonging to an independent farmer, and money was tight. It was cheaper to hire the local boys to manhandle the bales.

All of that made little difference to the serpent.

It lay unmoving, except for that tiny, almost unnoticeable *flick-flick-flick* of its tongue, tasting, smelling, tasting . . .

The dry cloud of pulverized straw that billowed behind the combine as its blades thrust *clack-clack-clack* through the field.

The hot oil spilling in greasy black droplets from the ancient baler's nearly worn-out engine.

3

The thick, black exhaust that stuttered from the flatbed's tailpipe whenever the driver hit the gas pedal.

The sweat of the men as they boosted bales on their knees high enough for the others in the flatbed to grab them and swing them onto the stacks.

The sweetish aroma of the wheat itself, bleeding from severed stalks, spilling its life-fluid onto the hot, thirsty ground.

The faint hint of moisture from the distant river.

The . . .

The black tongue flickered, paused, flickered again.

Ahhh. There it was . . .

The scent-taste-sound of something small scurrying this way, threading its way through the jungle of stalks and stems in a blind panic, racing through the stand of as-yet uncut grain, terrified beyond terror by the sounds and smells of the monster behind it that sliced and tore and shredded, that ruptured burrows with its massive tires and sent tiny communities of nervous rodents scampering for the safety of the untouched portions of the field.

A field mouse.

And it was *close*. Deliciously close.

The snake moved.

When it left the heat of the roadway, slid easily beneath the ramshackle barbed-wire fence that marked the boundary of the farmer's acreage, and entered the field, not a single stalk quivered to mark the hunter's passage from the bright sunlight into the shadows.

It made no noise as it insinuated its way toward the terrified mouse still running heedlessly away from the noise and confusion of the machines. Nothing would have noted its passing, brown on brown maneuvering through clots and small stones and broken, desiccated stalks.

The mouse careened forward. The machines' stench overcame its normally keen sense of smell; their noise drowned out any hint of warning from its almost preternaturally sharp hearing.

It jumped onto a small stone, paused for a fraction of a moment vainly sniffing the air, sniffing the air, then leaped . . .

Directly in front of the snake.

Suddenly only inches apart, both hunter and hunted froze.

Time seemed to have stopped.

Then, at the same instant, two things happened.

The tiny brown mouse leaped, straight upward at first, and then making as if to twist its body backward in a frantic attempt to escape, its long tail whipping sideways . . .

Just as the snake lunged, its blunt triangular head almost parallel to the ground, thrusting out from its coiled body almost too fast to follow with the naked eye. Jaws open and fangs extended, it struck the mouse just behind the neck, engulfing the mouse's entire head. The momentum carried the mouse onto its back, where it gave a single spasmodic shiver, went rigid with shock, and — almost miraculously, it seemed — flipped upward feet-first from the snake's abruptly open mouth. It contorted itself once in the air before landing on all four paws . . . again, directly in front of the snake, facing it.

In the instant it took for the mouse to

orient itself, the snake's head withdrew, as fluidly as quicksilver, into striking position.

But it did not strike.

Not immediately.

It could hear-taste-smell the mouse's terror, the frenzied, flurried beating of its tiny heart, the sound of its blood *thrum*-ing through its body, the scent of utter fear rising unbidden from its flesh.

It caught the mouse's wide-eyed gaze, caught it and held it, hypnotically.

It swayed its triangular head slightly to one side.

The mouse twitched just enough to follow the movement.

The snake swayed back.

The mouse's small, bead-like eyes followed.

The snake swayed sideways again.

Again the mouse's eyes followed.

The snake began to sway back to its original position — the mouse intent on the serpent's deep-set slitted eyes — when without a break in its rhythm, the snake surged forward, its head an impossible blur, jaws extended to their fullest revealing the satin-white lining of its mouth and its fangs protruding and deadly, this time pinioning the mouse, biting down hard, letting the venom drip into the mouse's quivering flesh.

And the battle — brief but epic — was over.

But the process — the almost interminable process — of consuming the mouse was only beginning.

1

'Hello?'

'Lynn, dear, is that you?'

'Victoria?' I darted a quick glance at the old-fashioned Big-Ben wind-up alarm clock on the pine nightstand. Its rigid arms pointed to 7:15. Not that long past dawn.

Even for what was essentially a farming community like Fox Creek, it was a bit early for a telephone call, especially a simple social call to exchange the latest recipes or gossip about the doings of wayward youngsters or brag about the splendid state of one's gladiolas.

'Victoria, are you all right?' My voice was harsher than usual, both because I had only been awake a few minutes and because of the sudden fear that made me sit bolt upright in bed.

'I'm just fine, dear.'

'Are you sure? It's only . . . '

'Yes, of course I'm sure. I just need to

ask a favor. It's about a friend of mine.'

By this time, I was on my feet, cell phone in hand, and on my way to the closet, mentally choosing which clothes I could throw on if Victoria Sears needed me right away.

'But you're okay?' I repeated. Victoria was, after all, well into her seventies, coming up on her eighties with a speed that I wasn't sure she herself sometimes recognized, and fiercely independent. Even knowing her for only a few weeks, I couldn't imagine anything short of a life-threatening emergency that would make the woman call — and call for *help* — this early. Victoria was a stickler for the proper forms.

Victoria laughed. It was a light, pleasant sound, like water running over stones in a creek bed in early spring. But we were already close enough friends for me to detect something more, a hint of darkness, beneath the sound. That small undercurrent frightened me.

'I'm fine. Really. But I do need your help with . . . with something that might be rather urgent.'

I had already pulled on a pair of jeans and was shifting the cell phone to my other hand so I could work my way into a blouse.

'What is it?'

'Well, a very dear friend of mine is . . . is in a bit of trouble, I think. I just got a call from Carver — the Ellises live next door to her — asking if I could get down there as soon as possible.'

'Do you need me to drive you?' Victoria owned a sturdy vehicle and was more than capable of driving herself anywhere she wanted. Perhaps she was more shaken up than I had imagined over her friend's difficulty — whatever it was — and didn't trust herself on the road.

'If you could I would greatly appreciate it. The Behemoth' — that was her pet name for her station wagon — 'is laid up at the moment. She's in the garage in town. If you could just pick me up and take me down-mountain and drop me off at the Ellises, I'd . . . '

'I'll be there in five minutes.'

'You don't need to hurry *too* fast. I don't think there is any real rush. Not any more. It's . . . well, I'm not sure there's really anything I can do, but I did tell Janet Ellis that I'd be there.'

'I'm almost out the door, Victoria,' I said, buttoning the last button on my blouse.

'Thank you, Lynn dear. I truly appreciate it.'

She hung up.

I rummaged around in my drawer for a thick pair of socks and dropped onto the rumpled bed to put them on. My high-topped hiking boots — a fashion statement I would never have dreamed of wearing before I arrived in Fox Creek only a couple of months earlier — were lying by the side of the bed where I had left them the previous afternoon after a long, luxurious tramp into the low mountains behind my cabin. Toppled onto their sides, the boots looked comically like a couple of exhausted soldiers taking a welcomed but unex- pected breather.

I didn't know what Victoria might need me for, but I knew enough about the area to come prepared. The last time I had shared an emergency with Victoria, we had had to hike up and down the mountains abutting her home twice, making one of the trips by flashlight long after dark, and this time I was determined to be ready for anything.

I grabbed a bagel from the refrigerator and gulped down a quick glass of icy milk. At the doorway, I nearly bolted through before I remembered to take my floppy straw hat down from the rack and jam it on my head. Estelle had instructed me to take a hat whenever I went anywhere, and her advice had proved useful several times now.

Okay — bagel, milk, hat. Check. And I was on my way.

Victoria's home — she called it a *cabin* but it was really much more than that — was only a mile and a quarter from the place I was renting from my mother's friends, Estelle and Edgar Van Etten. The first time I met Victoria, on that memorable day when Alix Macrorie's body had been discovered at the foot of Porcupine Falls, I had walked the distance. Physically, it had taken me the better part of half an hour but internally, the trek had seemed infinitely longer.

It had been the first anniversary of Terry and Shawn's deaths, and the last thing I had wanted was to let anyone else intrude on my private sorrows. But I had promised Estelle, and I had made the trip.

And in many ways, that short walk had saved my life.

Now I had a chance to repay Victoria in some small measure for what she had done for me that day.

It took a little more than five minutes of bouncing along the rutted road to get to Victoria's, but not much more. She was waiting for me at the gate that led from a low picket fence through a garden of carefully cultivated wild flowers to the front door of her house.

She was dressed in what I recognized as her get-out-and-get-to-work garb: loose jeans that would have looked absolutely ridiculous on any other woman her age but that seemed perfect for her; a riotously flowered blouse that must certainly have been handsewn but would have passed muster in any made-to-order store; sturdy boots of the same brand as my own (not a surprise, since she had taken me shopping shortly after the furor over Alix's death had subsided and instructed me in the relative merits of half a dozen possibilities); and her own wide-brimmed floppy hat. Her over-sized handbag hung loosely from its shoulder strap.

She waved a cheery greeting as I pulled up at the fence, but I thought I saw a certain grimness beneath her welcoming smile.

I had barely pulled to a stop before she was at the car door, had opened it, and was settling herself in the passenger seat, cinching her seat belt with a dexterity that would have put a woman thirty years her junior to shame.

With one hand she gestured — rather imperiously, perhaps, but I was used to her mannerisms — back down the road.

'Head on into town. The Ellises live just on the other side.'

Since the road dead-ended at Victoria's fence, it took me a couple of minutes to maneuver the car around, but finally we were aimed in the right direction. I hit the gas and we took off down the road.

Victoria didn't say much. At first she sat ramrod stiff, clutching the top of her handbag, which told me that she was far more concerned about whatever we were about to confront than she was willing to admit.

Something was wrong, *seriously* wrong.

I knew her well enough to understand that when it was time, she would tell me everything I needed to know. She was normally a fountain of information, at times down-right chatty, but today she seemed more taciturn than I had ever seen her.

We continued toward Fox Creek — 'down-mountain' as the natives would have said — until we passed Estelle and Edgar's place. Not too far beyond that point, the landscape altered noticeably. The pines and firs we had been threading through thinned out at the same time that the vista ahead broadened and flattened to reveal a long, fairly narrow valley between two stretches of mountains. It was perhaps ten miles across before the further range began again, first with a few small foothills — brown and sere in the late summer heat — then more abruptly with granite walls approaching the vertical and stands of evergreens clutching for life in the thin, scattered patches of soil.

In between lay acres of fertile farm land, sectioned here and there by graveled roads that gave access to a few distant homesteads, usually a house, a barn, and a few scattered outbuildings.

We passed one or two such places and, since the road was becoming both more level and more easily passable, I had begun to speed up a bit — nothing hair-raising, mind you, but substantially more than, say, what one would expect of a Sunday afternoon sightseeing jaunt.

Moving for nearly the first time since she sat down in the car, Victoria suddenly rested one hand on my arm and said, 'I think you'd better slow down, Lynn dear.'

'I'm not really speeding . . . ' I started to say but she tightened her grip on my arm with one hand and pointed toward the road ahead with the other.

'I really think you should slow down. You wouldn't want to hit that.'

I stared ahead. And saw nothing, except a long, thin twig straddling the middle of the road.

A four-foot-long twig . . . that abruptly moved.

I must have nearly screamed — a combination of taut nerves because of the as-yet unnamed emergency that was so serious that Victoria didn't even want to speak about it, and the sudden movement ahead as the twig raised its narrow, glistening head toward us and began to coil the rest of its long, lithe body.

'It's nothing to worry about, dear. Just slow down and give it a chance to save face and get away. Remember, it's more frightened of us than we are of it.'

Yeah, right.

I slowed.

Almost as soon as the car began to lose forward momentum, the twig — that is, the *snake* uncoiled and, moving in sinuous curves that held a curiously off-putting beauty and grace, slipped over the rough ruts and disappeared into a thick bank of white-flowered vegetation in the borrow-pit.

I knew those plants.

Queen Anne's Lace.

After Victoria's and my earlier experiences, I recognized the good Queen, and I tendered Her Majesty a good deal more respect and attention because of that. She and her dastardly cousin, Devil's Plague — more familiarly known in the Fox Creek area as Western Water Hemlock, a fatally poisonous plant.

But that, as they always say in the books, is another story.

Without realizing it, I had been holding my breath the whole time, until the smooth tip of the snake's tail finally disappeared into the shadows. I let out the pent-up air with a distinct *whoosh* and turned to face Victoria.

'That wasn't a rattlesnake, was it? I didn't see any rattles or anything.'

She laughed again, the same water-over-stones light rippling laugh that still held a hint of something shadowy.

'That, my dear, was merely a king snake. Poor fellow was probably just

19

resting after a long night hunting, and our noise startled it. By now it's probably halfway home for a long day's sleep, or maybe scouting out in the marshy areas for a final bit of a snack.'

'Poisonous?'

'Not at all. In fact, most of the boys around here, and probably more girls than would care to admit to it, have had a baby king snake as a pet at one time or another. For insects and worms and birds' eggs — when they are lucky enough to find any — they are lethal. For us humongous humans, absolutely harmless.'

I couldn't help it. In spite of the growing sense of something being wrong somewhere, I laughed this time.

Laughed and shook my head.

'I think, Victoria, that I've had just about enough of your royalty up here in the mountains.'

She looked momentarily puzzled.

'King snakes scaring me half to death. And Queen-weeds trying to poison people.'

'Queen . . . ? Oh, yes. Right.' She

smiled to let me know she caught the joke. But it was a thin smile.

We were passing the final few patches of open field before entering Fox Creek proper. We clattered over an ancient iron bridge that spanned Fox Creek — unlike so many places back home, especially housing developments with pretentions to grandeur, up here, if something was called 'Creek' you could pretty well bet that there would be a creek somewhere nearby.

The water was lower than it had been in early June but still higher than would be considered normal for this time of year, I was told by the folks who had spent their lives here. Summer heat coupled with the final spate of irrigation before harvests had siphoned off some of the earlier flow. Rocks showed in the middle of the channel, mossy and green a few weeks ago but now looking as if they had been thatched with ragged, clotted straw.

In a truly dry year, the locals assured me, Fox Creek could look like nothing more or less than a barely connected series of mudholes. When that happened, it was anything but a glamor spot.

When we hit the paved road on the other side of the bridge, we officially entered Fox Creek.

It's a small place, really, especially to anyone used to the 'big city' as I was, but I was surprised how long it took us to pass through four of its five intersections. Luckily, the lights were green. As far as I could see, there was no other traffic.

At the city limits, the state road turns into Main Street, and continues under that name to the far side of the town, then it resumes its original moniker.

We didn't get that far.

'Turn here,' Victoria instructed as we approached the fifth stop light. In 'town talk,' that would be Avenue C, but again, once we passed the edge of town, it would continue as County Road 5A.

'Ellises live along here, about three miles farther on.'

We drove in silence. The county road was in better condition than the gravel track leading up to Victoria's house, so there were fewer rattles and bumps. We didn't see any more snakes, but I noticed a covey of redwing blackbirds perched on the cattails that grow in wild profusion between the roadbed and the nearest fields. The ground here would be swampy, damp even in August.

Once a quail darted into the middle of the road, hesitated for an instant when I realized we were there, then, instead of dashing ahead and getting across in plenty of time for us to miss it, it suddenly decided to go back the way it had come. It spun around so fast — its low-slung, plump body on those ridiculously frail-looking stick legs — that it nearly toppled over.

My front tires missed it by no more than a yard.

Foolish bird.

Victoria seemed not to have noticed the moment of comic by-play. Her hand was gripping the flap on her handbag again, and she was staring out the passenger window as if there were something of life-or-death seriousness happening in the passing fields.

'It's not much further,' Victoria said a

few moments later. She pointed with one hand, finally releasing her grasp on her handbag. 'Turn in at the first place. Down there.'

Up ahead I could see two houses — traditional clapboard farmhouses, two stories high, with deeply set wrap-around porches, huge maples shading the front yards and gravel driveways leading to side doors. The two houses were perhaps two hundred yards apart. They might belong to different families — and from what little I could glean from Victoria's few remarks, they did — but they were alike as twins.

Form follows function, probably. Both were at least half a century old, perhaps older.

We turned in at the first drive.

Someone was waiting for us at the end.

I must admit that my heart thumped a bit faster for an instant when I recognized Carver Ellis.

Not that there is anything between us . . . romantically, I mean. Even if I were in the market for a boyfriend — much less a 'significant other' (how I hate that phrase)

— there would be nothing between us. Chronologically, he's still pretty much just a kid, nearly a decade younger than my own twenty-nine years, but at times he seems even younger than that. I think there may be something developmentally not-quite-right. He's not slow mentally, nothing like that, but occasionally there is the sense about him that he's not as mature, not as adaptable to change or challenges, not as . . . well, not as *adult* as his years would suggest.

He's often more child-like than I expect, frequently surprising me.

Not childish. Just child-like. Innocent.

Well, I suppose that *innocent* is not exactly the right word. But perhaps you know what I mean.

Still, my heart flipped over one or two beats when I saw him standing there, waiting for us.

Because Carver Ellis is *beautiful*.

I know I shouldn't use that word for a young man, but it is the only one that truly fits. Muscular in all the right ways, the ways that suggest hard work, and lots of it, rather than narcissistic afternoon visits to a gym. Add to that a perfectly chiseled face. Startlingly blue eyes. Blond hair bleached almost white by daily exposure to the sun. Deep, even tan — I knew what his torso looked like because I had seen him once or twice shirtless as he worked around Victoria's place, but I strongly suspected that not too far south of his waistline the tan would suddenly vanish.

Not that I ever expected, or in fact *wanted*, to actually verify that by personal observation, but I knew that he supported his widowed mother and that there were more than enough calls for his skill as a handyman to keep him too busy to lay around in the sun working on a tan.

Yes, the boy was beautiful, but as I drove closer I noted something else.

This morning, underneath his tan, his skin was almost deathly pallid. His face seemed drawn and his hair was disheveled, as if he had jumped out of bed and finger-combed it on his way out rather than spending any time in front of a mirror.

And, closer yet, I could see that his

hands were trembling.

'Victoria,' I said, keeping my eyes on Carver's distraught face, 'what's wrong?'

'I don't know for sure. Carver can be . . . well, *scattered* when he's worried. And right now, I think he's plenty worried.'

She was out of the car before I turned the engine off, standing next to Carver with her hand on his shoulder . . . a bit of a reach, actually, since he was a good head taller than she was.

I didn't hear what she asked him, but by the time he answered I was almost even with Victoria and I heard him.

I heard him just fine.

'It's Rick Johansson. From next door.

'He's dead.'

2

'Dead! Oh, Carver, no.' Victoria's voice sounded as distressed as I felt. She might have added, 'Not again!' but she didn't.

I didn't know anything about Rick Johansson, had never even heard his name until that moment, so news of his death, while sad, didn't touch me very deeply. But I knew Carver, and I knew from first-hand experience how he responded to death.

I even knew how he reacted when he was charged with *causing* a death.

I had seen him accused of murder.

He didn't deserve to go through that again.

'Are you sure?' Victoria was asking.

Carver simply nodded, his eyes wide with . . . with what? Sorrow? Loss? Fear? Dread?

I couldn't read him.

'Where is Greta?'

'Inside, with Mom,' Carver said,

gesturing with his head over his shoulder. 'Mom didn't want her alone in their house with . . . with Rick's . . . with Rick.'

Victoria squeezed Carver's shoulder lightly and went on into the house. I heard her call out 'Janet? Greta?' and then the door banged shut.

'I didn't know what else to do,' Carver said, as if he had to explain himself to me. 'It just seemed automatic to call Miz Sears. I figured she would know . . . '

'I'm sure that was exactly the right thing to do,' I said. My heart went out to him. 'Was . . . uh, Rick was it?'

Carver nodded again.

'Was Rick a close friend? Somebody you knew from school?'

He shook his head this time.

'I didn't really know him that well. He's only lived with Miz Johan . . . with his grandma for about a year. He was pretty much a loner. But sometimes we worked together on jobs.

'We were helping Mr. Nielson — Tom Nielson, that is — put up his grain yesterday. And he called me last night from Land's End to come pick him up.

Said he didn't feel well.'

Carver seemed to shudder.

'Let's go on in, shall we?'

He looked up and blinked, as if seeing me for the first time.

'Right. I should be in there to help Mom. And Miz Johansson.'

He led the way through the door, which opened onto the kitchen. In the next room — probably the living room — I could hear the low murmur of women's voices, the kind of sounds that warn of illness or death or other tragedy.

By the time we entered, Victoria had clearly taken charge. She was standing near a low sofa on which two women were sitting. One held a fragile tea cup that occasionally clinked against the saucer in her other hand. She looked to be about fifty. From the blond hair, blue eyes, and strong features, I could tell that this must be Janet Ellis, Carver's mother.

The other woman was much older. She looked even older than Victoria, but that impression might have been wrong since, where Victoria even in her seventies was a fountain of energy and activity, this woman — Mrs. Johansson — looked washed out, drained, as fragile as the china tea cup and saucer sitting untouched on the low table in front of her. In fact, I think the tea cup would have survived a sharp blow more easily than this woman would have.

Her hair was wispy, almost like a halo-effect, and that odd yellow-white that sometimes happens with old people and that makes them look faded and ill even if they are in the best of health. Her eyes were red-rimmed and watery, and her lips, pursed and tight, nonetheless quivered with each thin breath she drew.

She was wearing a worn chenille robe that had to have been as old as I was. I wouldn't even have begun to guess what color it might have started out life as, or if it had ever been printed with a bright, cheerful pattern. Her feet were thrust into shapeless scuffs that had likewise long since lost any hint of color.

Victoria had knelt beside her and laid her hand on the other woman's knee.

'Can you talk now, Greta? Can you tell us anything?'

Greta Johansson put a lace-edged handkerchief to her eyes and dabbed before nodding.

'Victoria? Is that you?' The voice quavered and the hand that she laid over Victoria's shook violently.

'Yes, dear, it's me. Janet called me.'

'Janet?'

'I'm right here, too, Miz Johansson. We are going to take care of everything. Don't you worry.' Janet Ellis leaned across and patted the old hand that lay atop Victoria's. For an awful moment, I was reminded of Shawn and the rest of his little friends grasping the handle of a baseball bat to determine first ups, and found that I had to blink back a few tears of my own.

Shawn was my baby and he was dead. Almost two years dead. As was Terry. I could feel for this woman — a woman I had never seen — in her grief and confusion and loss.

'Janet? Did Rick let you in? I didn't hear you knock? Why didn't I hear you knock?'

'No, Miz Johansson, Rick is . . . '

Victoria shook her head.

'Greta, dear,' she said, drawing the old woman's attention to her and fixing Greta's eyes with her own. 'We are in Janet's home. Carver brought you over here this morning. And Janet fixed you this nice cup of tea. Do you remember that?'

'Tea?' She reached irresolutely toward the cup, then drew back her hand. 'Yes. That's right. Janet made me tea. And Carver woke me up and told me that I was to come with him. He came into my bedroom and woke me up. He helped me put my robe on over my night dress.'

Now her hand rose to her throat and clutched at the robe's lapels, pinning them closed.

'He shouldn't have done that, you know. Come into a lady's bedroom like that. If Eric knew what . . . '

For a moment there had been a flash of something like life in her eyes, but at the mention of her grandson's name, the flash expired. She slumped.

'Is Eric dead? Victoria, is it true? Is my little Eric really dead?'

Victoria glanced at Carver, who nodded once then dropped his eyes to the floor.

'Yes, dear, I'm afraid he is.'

'What happened? Do you know what happened? He was fine yesterday at lunch. I didn't see him afterward because he had to get to work but he was fine he ate a whole sandwich that wasn't like him at all he's usually such a finicky eater and I was so proud . . . '

She hid her head in her hands.

Victoria patted her shoulder in the time-honored 'There, there' movement that only certain grandmothers and certain women who should have been grandmothers but never were can quite carry off.

Victoria could.

I could see the older woman's shoulders relaxing under Victoria's touch.

'No, dear. I don't know anything yet. But I will find out. I promise you. We'll see that everything is taken care of.'

'Victoria, is that you?' The querulous note was back. 'Where am I?'

Victoria nodded to Janet Ellis, who slid across the sofa and put her arm around the older woman, drawing her in closer as if she were a small child that needed desperately to be consoled.

I could hear her whispering to Greta, not words really, but sounds of comfort that were apparently enough for the older woman.

Victoria turned to face Carver and me.

'Carver, what can you tell us?'

'Not much. I was supposed to get him up. We were scheduled to go by Mr. Nielson's place this morning, to talk to him about Rick's getting his job back because the accident really *wasn't* his fault' — I wanted to interrupt to ask 'What accident?' but found that I couldn't just then, and I figured that we would get all of the details in good time — 'it just happened, I think, you know, and then after noon we . . . that is, I was going to . . . '

'Carver, focus, dear.'

'Yeah. Anyway I told him last night I would wake him up because he was . . . well, he was pretty drunk and, I don't know, maybe wasted, I'm not sure.'

He caught a glance from Victoria and

swallowed hard, visibly pulling himself back on track.

'So I went over this morning and the side door was unlocked like he said it would be, like it always is, you know, because out here we don't usually have any trouble with . . . The door was unlocked, and I didn't knock because I knew that his grand . . . that Miz Johansson sometimes didn't get to sleep until really late and wouldn't want to be waked this early. So I went on in.

'He was still in bed. He was just sprawled there, no quilt, no sheet, just like he had been last night when I brought him home. He hadn't even taken his clothes off. He was just *there*. And I could tell that he was . . . that he was dead.' The boy almost broke into tears. As it was he had to blink rapidly several times to clear his vision.

'So I went right downstairs and woke Miz Johansson and helped her get dressed . . . and I didn't see anything I shouldn't, you know I wouldn't do anything like that, don't you . . . ' The overt plea for understanding on even this one small point was heart-breaking.

'Of course, Carver dear. But you must concentrate. You woke Eric's grandmother and . . . '

'I woke her up and helped her dress and helped her get over here and by then Mom was up and I told her what had happened and she took Miz Johansson in with her and set her down on the couch and told me to call for help, so I called for you because I knew that you would know what we should do.'

'You did fine. That couldn't have been easy for you.'

Carver nodded again, whether in agreement with the latter statement or gratitude for the former I couldn't tell.

'What did Deputy Wroten say when you called the substation?'

'I didn't call him.'

For the first time, Victoria's sense of command faltered.

'He wasn't at the substation? Was Deputy Allen there instead?'

Carver blanched even further at the mention of the younger deputy's name; they did not get along well at all. Too much past history.

'I didn't call him, either. I didn't call the cops at all.'

Normally Victoria might have corrected Carver's usage, since she herself insisted on *deputy* or *police officer*, but she let the smaller infraction slide and zeroed in on the larger.

'Carver, did you even *call* the substation?'

'No. I didn't think of it at first, all I could think of was that Miz Victoria would know what to do, and then later, while I was waiting for you to get here, I . . . I didn't want to call them. I didn't want to talk to them.'

'I suppose you didn't call the coroner's office, either.' It was not a question.

Carver shook his head.

'Or Doc Anderson's?'

Again, the silent answer.

'Good Lord,' Victoria murmured almost under her breath — it was as close as she would come to a profanity . . . and obscenities were utterly beneath her dignity.

'Well, it can't be helped now. Carver, you come with me. And you too, Lynn dear, if you don't mind.'

'Sure,' I said, not quite knowing what I was letting myself in for.

'Janet, while we're gone, do you think you could call the substation and let them know? Someone should get out here as quickly as possible.'

Janet Ellis looked up from the couch. The older woman didn't move. She seemed almost asleep.

'I'll help Greta into the guest room and then call. Where will you be? Over there?'

'Yes.'

And then, for the first time, I had a clear inkling of what was going to happen.

3

We drove to the house next door.

Turning down the long gravel-strewn driveway felt eerily familiar . . . the same *crunch* of tires on dirty grey stone, the same beds of roses bordering both sides of the drive, differing from those along the Ellises' driveway only in color — Janet's, which I had barely noticed earlier that morning, had been white, while Greta's were pink shaded with yellow, what used to be called Peace roses.

Otherwise the two places seemed almost identical.

When we approached closer, however, I could see signs that things were not quite the same. The clapboard panels on Greta's house were beginning to peel and splinter, as if they had not been tended for some years. The house needed a new coat of paint and the windows were dusty, suggesting that they hadn't been washed since the last rainstorm some time before.

The kitchen door was just as dilapidated as the rest of the house. Where Janet's had opened silently, mute testimony to Carver's carpentering skill and his resolute concern for keeping his mother's house in good shape, Greta's door squealed and balked. The noise grated on our ears, especially in the quiet of the early morning.

'I tried to come by when I could and take care of things,' Carver muttered as if in apology, 'but I haven't had much time lately.'

'Didn't Eric . . . ' I began.

'Most people called him 'Rick,'' Carver said. 'Except for his grandmother. And Miz Sears. They always called him 'Eric.' And he wasn't much . . . he didn't . . . ' Carver faltered.

'He was not much into manual labor,' Victoria completed. 'Unless he was paid for it.' She glanced quickly around the place, taking in the shaggy grass, the scraggly appearance of the un-pruned roses. 'Greta thought that he might learn to like working with his hands, but he never did.'

I had more questions but now didn't seem like the right time.

The kitchen smelled.

It wasn't rank or anything like that. There was just a trace of unpleasant odors — the garbage can by the door was covered and clean, but it smelled like it should have been taken out a day or two before. There were several pots and pans stacked on the counter, their contents crusted and dried. They should have been long since washed and put away.

And the place smelled *old*.

You know what I mean. It's really nothing quite identifiable. Just an occasional whiff of something slightly medicinal, something nearly like talc or baby powder, mixed with the slightest suggestion of staleness.

Victoria's house would never smell *old*, no matter how many more years she spent there.

Greta's house had probably smelled that way for decades. Victoria had mentioned on the way over from Janet's that Arnie Johansson, Greta's husband, had died some years before of a particularly virulent cancer. First they had noted a few slight swellings in his armpits and groin. By the time the couple — then in their sixties — had finally overcome their fears sufficiently to visit a doctor, the only news they received was bad.

Mr. Johansson was given three to six months to live, a year at the absolute most.

He had lasted fewer than six weeks.

Basically, once he received the word, he had given up. He went home that day, Victoria said, sat down in an old bentwood rocker, and had barely moved again — had barely even spoken again — until Greta had made him a bed on the living room sofa.

There he had died.

The house still carried the lingering scent of death.

Or perhaps I just imagined it.

The living room was as disheveled-looking as the kitchen had been. A newspaper lay open on the carpet. A man's T-shirt hung limply over the back of an armchair. An old-fashioned knitting bag crouched by the foot of the sofa, its balls of yarn tangled around a bit of half-completed work.

Everything looked as if Greta, like her husband before her, had faced something unpleasant and unwanted and had simply given up.

'He's upstairs.'

Carver's voice was startlingly loud. The only other sound was the hollow, solemn *tick-tick-tick* of a grandmother clock on the mantle. I glanced over.

It read half past three.

Greta had apparently been careful to keep it wound but had not cared enough to correct the time.

'Right, then,' Victoria said. She led the way through the living room toward a staircase in the far corner.

The stairs were as old and worn as the rest of the house. The treads were unpolished, uncarpeted, splintering along the leading edge. I would not have cared to go up or down them barefoot. There was only one rail and it was smooth, more from constant wear than from any particular care. It felt slightly greasy to the touch.

At the top of the stairs, Victoria paused and motioned for Carver to lead the way.

The first two doors were closed. Guest rooms perhaps, or simply bedrooms once intended to be filled with the playful offspring of the original builders — always assuming that the Johanssons hadn't actually built the place themselves — but now empty and dusty, the air inside hot and musty and thick.

The third door was ajar.

Carver halted outside the door. His hand reached out as if to push it further open, then dropped to his side.

'That's all right, dear,' Victoria said and she stepped past him into the room.

'Oh.'

That was all she said. But it was enough.

I looked through the doorway.

The room was a shambles, even discounting the still figure of the young man lying on the bed, the blood that had seeped from an unknown number of wounds both seen and unseen staining the yellowing sheet beneath the body and already beginning to crust. What had once — not that long ago — been startlingly red was now rusty-looking and brown.

The rest of the room looked as if it had been, as the police might have said, 'tossed.'

Clothing lay everywhere, scattered on the single dingy orange dresser that looked as if it had to have been picked up in a moment of utmost need at some garage sale or second-hand flea market. Most of the drawers hung partially open, and the one that did not, fit badly into the frame, leaving thick lines of darkness surrounding the front. One pull was missing; the raw ends of a screw protruded an inch or so outward.

More clothing covered the single chair, a straight-backed, uncomfortable piece of furniture that looked as if it might serve more adequately as a repository for soiled underwear and filthy-soled socks than as a place to sit. I half believed that I could smell the dirty laundry from where I stood, clear across the room.

The closet door stood open, revealing a tangle of old-fashioned wire hangers jutting from the rod, as if whatever had been hanging there had been torn away, even *violently* torn away. A T-shirt — with the faded imprint 'Go, Longhorns' visible on the back, hung from the top corner of the door. Most of the clothing that the closet was originally designed to hold was apparently piled pell-mell on the floor.

The carpet was almost invisible beneath a layer of cast-off jeans, several sweat-shirts, at least a dozen shoes — all of them sneakers in various stages of disintegration — no two of which seemed like pairs, and a sprinkling of fast-food wrappers, stained pizza boxes, and assorted other detritus sprinkled like inedible condiments across the mess.

Only one piece of furniture looked untouched, although even there the top was laden with unidentifiable lumps and piles. On the four shelves beneath, rows of books stood, to all appearances untouched, certainly unread.

Room stank of dirty socks and old pizza . . . and, faintly, of urine and something worse.

'What happened here?' I think my voice

must have communicated how stunned I was. 'Was he robbed, do you think?'

'No, ma'am. It always looked like this. Sometimes when I would come by and his grandmother was already up, I would hear her screaming at him to clean up after himself. But he never would.'

'Nor will he ever again,' Victoria said quietly, bringing us back to the present and the horrible fact that the mess, however appalling, was the least of our current concerns.

At a small gesture from her, Carver and I both entered the room, taking care not to tread on anything, if possible, and standing as far from the bed as we could.

Even that precaution was not particularly helpful, since the room was smallish and the bed stuck out from the wall like a rumpled peninsula in a sea of trash.

Victoria stepped closer, however, like us trying not to disturb anything. I could almost read her mind: 'We'll have to be able to tell the police that this was the way we found it . . . but *I* need a closer look.'

She stood next to the bed, occasionally

leaning forward slightly.

Eric Johansson lay stretched out on the bed. There was no pillow — it had somehow ended up on the floor under the half-closed window. The only bedding still on the bed was the single sheet on which the body rested. The remainder was twisted and knotted on the floor at the foot of the bed, as if at some time he had had a truly bad night and kicked off the other sheet and the thin, worn quilt.

I didn't think that it had happened last night. There were a couple of odds and ends of clothing on top of the bedding, including a black leather belt studded with what looked like three rows of tiny silver pyramids along its entire length, that coiled on itself like a snake, its metal buckle half-hidden and glinting sinisterly in the light.

'Was this the way you left him when you put him to bed?' Victoria did not turn to face Carver but we knew that she was talking to him.

'Yeah. Pretty much. I got his boots and socks off,' he said, pointing to a pair of mud-caked books nearly hidden beneath the bed. 'And his shirt.' This time he indicated a crumpled wad of plaid near the head of the bed. 'It was warm last night. I didn't want to undress him anymore so I left his jeans and T-shirt on, and besides he was almost asleep by that time. And I didn't think he would need to be covered up.'

Victoria nodded.

By this time, both Carver and I had shuffled a bit nearer the bed and could see the body — which had been partially hidden by Victoria standing between us and it — clearly and completely.

The young man — the *boy* really, since he was barely out of his teens, I would guess, if that — was flat on his back, both arms straight along his side, as if he had been arranged that way. I didn't ask Carver if he had done that.

One hip was canted slightly, and his right leg, the one nearest us, was bent at the knee.

Victoria pointed to the boy's jeans.

'Did that happen last night?'

'What?'

'Those rips along the knees. I can tell

that he was in a fight of some sort before you brought him home' — she didn't mention the alternative . . . that *Carver* had beaten the boy — 'and I need to know if that was when he tore his pants.'

'Uh . . . no. No, all of his jeans were like that. He wore them like that on purpose. I don't know if he did it himself or bought them already torn.'

I leaned in a bit more and studied the leg.

The flesh, where it was exposed by a long ragged rip that extended from seam to seam and was feathered along the edges until the remaining thread looked like small fluffs of dirty cotton, resembled raw meat loaf gone bad. The knee itself was swollen, taut and shiny. The skin along the upper surface was raw, scored, and bloody, crusted, with bits of something that might have been gravel, or just clotted blood, caught in the scabs. It must have been painful . . . except that Rick Johansson was dead and would never feel it or anything else again.

'What about the other leg?' Victoria asked.

I was in the best position, so I leaned a bit further over the body.

The left leg was straight, so the tear — artfully arranged, apparently to give the wearer of the jeans just the right touch of insouciance about things sartorial — was nearly closed. It was harder to see beneath to the knee and I didn't want to pull the material away to check any more closely. But . . .

'I think so. At any rate, there is blood on the denim, and the edges where the jeans are torn look like . . . like the fringe on a cheap rug after it's been on the floor for a while . . . ,' I finished, rather lamely.

'Yes,' Victoria said. 'I see.'

'But what about the rest, the . . . the cuts and bruises?' I was standing at the foot of the bed but I could see the boy's head well enough to tell that something dreadful had happened to him, and not that long before.

'Yes,' Victoria said, but now she turned toward Carver. 'What about the rest?'

Carver looked distinctly uncomfortable, as if the thought had just struck him that *he* might be held accountable for the shape the body was in.

'Well, part of it came from yesterday afternoon, I know that. He and Mr . . . he got into a fight at the field where we were working and . . . someone gave him a good right across the jaw. It knocked him ass over tea kett . . . ' Carver stopped abruptly.

'I'm familiar with the expression, dear. So don't worry about your language right now. But I'm afraid that you are going to have to tell us . . . or at least tell *someone* . . . who was fighting with this boy.'

Carver swallowed hard but did not speak.

'Yes, I can see a large bruise along the jawbone,' Victoria said, pointing with one finger — a remarkably calm and steady finger. 'That would be where he was first struck.

'But what about the rest?' and here she gestured toward a wicked looking cut over Rick's right eye, another along the curve of his cheek next to his eye, and a huge bruise on his temple. Against the pallor of the bloodless flesh, the cuts looked like living things, white-edged lips caught half-open in some horrible kind of stasis. The bruise was vivid purple.

'I don't know,' Carver said simply. 'He was like that when I picked him up last night at the bar.'

'Did he say anything about another fight?'

'No. Actually, he never said anything much about anything. Just grunted and moaned now and then when I loaded him into the car. By the time I got him here and up the stairs — now that was a real chore — he was pretty much out of it.'

'I wonder,' Victoria said, more to herself than to any of us.

She caught the lower edge of the boy's T-shirt with one finger and gently lifted.

'Oh no,' I breathed, not able to stop myself.

'Shit,' Carver said at the same time, then: 'Sorry, Miz Sears, Miz Hanson.'

Neither of us responded to his apology. We were mesmerized, I think, by what Victoria had just revealed.

4

The T-shirt had once been white but was now torn and dirty, with smudges across the chest and shoulders, a long rip along the ribs, and more than a spattering of blood down the front. From the evidence of the sheet beneath the body, it was saturated with blood on the back as well.

I suppose that we had all assumed that the blood was from the head wounds, that at some time the night before Rick Johansson had wiped his face with his T-shirt, trying to clean up after the beating he had received at the hands of an unknown assailant ... or unknown assailants.

What we hadn't expected was the massive bruising along his stomach and ribcage. It looked as if he had been treated like a punching bag, or perhaps he had been knocked to the ground and then kicked in the ribs by someone wearing heavy shoes.

Or boots.

'Do you know anything about this, Carver?'

'No, Miz Sears. Absolutely not. All I knew was that Rick called me late last night to have me pick him up from Land's End . . . '

'That's a rather sleazy bar on the far side of town, Lynn dear. It has quite an unsavory reputation. Or so I'm told. I've never been there.'

I couldn't help asking: 'Did Rick go there often?'

'I don't know. He'd never called me from there before,' Carver said, his forehead creased in thought. 'I wouldn't have expected to find him there, and I know that if Miz Johansson had known that he was hanging out there last night she would have pitched a grade-A-one fit.'

'No,' Victoria said. 'I'm sure you're right. Greta would never have countenanced her grandson frequenting a place like that. It would have killed her to find out.'

She stood for a long while musing

about something. Once she leaned over and took a closer look at the torn up flesh revealed by the rip over the knee.

'I wonder if we would find bruising and cuts on his upper thighs as well. If he was down, and someone kicked at him, it would probably show on his legs.'

Again, it looked as if she was thinking about something.

Then: 'No, we had better not. Wiser to leave him as he is.'

'Should we maybe cover him, you know, with a sheet or something?' Carver looked around as if a pristine sheet might suddenly materialize in front of us.

'No,' I said quietly. 'I think it would be best for us to leave him just like this. That way . . . '

'*Police! Anyone here? Hello!*'

All three of us jumped as if we had stepped in unison onto a downed power line and received the shock of our lives. Victoria's hand went up to her throat, and for an awful moment I was reminded of Greta's tremulous hand clutching at the lapels of her robe. Carver went even whiter, his eyes darting around the room, making him look like a cornered rabbit desperate to find an escape.

Victoria recovered first.

'We're up here. There are three of us. Lynn Hanson, Carver Ellis, and myself, Victoria Sears.'

A moment later a man in uniform stood in the doorway. His hand was resting on his holster. He looked like he would draw on us if we even sneezed.

Then he relaxed — slightly but visibly — and dropped his hand.

'Miz Sears,' he said slowly. 'I might have known.'

It was Deputy Allen.

The last time I had seen him was when Alix Macrorie had died. He had tried to arrest Carver and . . .

'My, my,' he said, looked from one of us to the other. 'What have we here?'

He smiled. It was a singularly discomfiting smile. It didn't reach his eyes, which glared at each of us in turn, unblinking and cold.

'Interesting little tableaux we have, isn't it? Looks mighty familiar to me.'

'Be that as it may, Deputy Allen,'

58

Victoria said, rather stiffly it seemed. 'What we have here is a young man who unfortunately passed away during the night.'

Allen moved across the room to stand at the head of the bed, next to Victoria. I noticed that he made no effort to avoid treading on the clothing and other detritus scattered on the floor. His boots came down hard on something lumpy under a dirty shirt, and the something cracked as if it had broken. Allen didn't seem to hear, or if he did, he didn't care.

I also noticed that Carver had slipped behind me and now stood on the opposite side of the bed, near the foot. It was as far from the deputy as he could reasonably get without drawing too much attention to himself.

Carver was still white, but now a faint pink flush was creeping up from his neck and his breathing had abruptly grown more rapid, noisy.

I wished heartily that Deputy Wroten, the officer in charge at the substation, had been the one to answer this call.

'His name,' Victoria said into the

silence, 'was Eric Johansson. He was . . . '

'Yeah, I know him. He's been living with Miz Johansson for about a year now. Moved up here after his parents were killed in a plane crash. He's been into the office to see us a couple of times. By *our* invitation,' he added pointedly.

'Ah. Anything . . . um . . . serious?' Victoria sounded diffident but I could tell that she was under some strain. 'Greta . . . his grandmother, that is, is an old friend of mine. She never spoke of any particular . . . trouble.'

'No, she wouldn't, would she. She's not that kind. And no, there was nothing that serious. Mostly kid stuff.'

'Can you tell . . . ?'

'No, ma'am, I can't. And even if I could, I probably wouldn't. You see, I don't know what happened out here last night. All I know is that Miz Ellis just called to say that young Johansson here was dead and that his grandmother was at her house but the body was still over here. I took the call. Here I am.

'And I find you three clustered around the body like . . . well, clustered around the body. And I find it interesting that at least one of you has been a . . . *ahem*' — he cleared his throat, rather theatrically given the circumstances — 'a *person of interest* in a previous mysterious death.'

Good grief! I thought. The man is *enjoying this!*

So far, not a question of any substance about the dead boy, just innuendos and nuanced comments directed at *us.*

I would have glanced at Carver to see how he was taking things but didn't dare. The last thing Allen needed was any provocation to make him notice Carver.

But, of course, I didn't have to offer one.

Allen's eyes were already glaring across the bed, toward the foot, where Carver was standing.

'Where were you last night, *Mr.* Ellis.' Allen came down on Carver's last name, stamping it with an unwarranted freight of suspicion.

'Wait a minute. You can't . . . ' Carver turned dead white again and backed up a step, as if proximity to the body might somehow infect him with . . . with what, with *guilt?*

'Nobody's doing anything, son,' Allen said, his tone countering any sympathetic feelings the words might have spawned. 'Just a simple question. Where were you?'

Carver glanced frantically at Victoria, as if she were the only bastion of hope in a hopeless world.

She nodded fractionally. And Allen caught the movement. I could almost hear his thoughts: *That's right, sonny-boy, check with the old lady since your own ma isn't here. Get someone on your side before you come clean.*

Carver swallowed hard.

'I was . . . I was just telling Miz Sears here that he . . . that Rick called me late last night to ask for a ride home from Land's End.'

'And did you pick him up?'

'Yes, sir.'

'Was he all right?'

'Well, he looked pretty beat up. Like you see him.'

'And you did nothing to help, what . . . *improve* his looks? You didn't get in a lick or two?'

'No.' Carver's voice angled up toward

an adolescent pitch. He was frightened about something.

'You two were just the best of pals, then.'

'Yes . . . No . . . I mean, we . . . '

'Maybe you were both sniffing after the same girl. Maybe you have a few words and . . . '

'No. I don't have a girlfriend.'

'Ri-i-ight. You don't have a girlfriend, do you? She's dead, isn't she . . . '

Carver made as if to leap over the bed — body and all — to get at Allen. Victoria halted him with a gesture.

'Carver! Focus.'

She turned to face Allen, her hands on her hips in an imperious stance.

'And you . . . you come here with . . . '

'I have a few ideas about what happened here, Miz Sears, and . . . '

'I'll just bet you have a few ideas.' Victoria's voice was sharper than I had ever heard it.

'And you can just keep those few ideas to yourself until you get one more thing. One tiny little thing.'

'And what would that be, ma'am.' The

sarcasm was so thick I could have cut it . . . if I'd had a knife.

'Proof.'

'Of what?'

'Of *anything*,' Victoria snapped back. 'Right now, all you have is this poor boy's body lying here on the bed and you are doing *nothing at all* to figure out what happened. Figure that out first. Then figure out *who did it*.'

Allen simply stared at her for a long while.

'You're right,' he said finally. 'First things first. Then' — he shot a glare at Carver that promised more pain and humiliation for the younger man — 'then we'll take care of the rest of the business.'

5

On Deputy Allen's instructions, the three of us went downstairs, leaving the body as we had found it. Even the hem of the T-shirt that Victoria had lifted to examine the abdomen had fallen precisely back to the same place, concealing the extent of Eric's injuries. I don't think Deputy Allen had seen the massive bruising . . . yet.

I was sure he would soon.

Even before we reached the landing, I heard Allen on his radio talking to someone — another deputy or the dispatcher at the substation. I only got his end of the conversation, but I figured out that he was calling for backup or something.

We reached the bottom of the stairs when the lights began — *Flash! Flash! Flash!* — spaced with a minute or so between. He was probably photographing the scene.

The death scene.

The *crime* scene.

It all felt so familiar, even though none of the details were.

'Carver,' Victoria said in a low voice, not quite a whisper but noticeably softer than her usual speaking tone, 'I want you to go on home now, be with Mrs. Johansson and your mother. You hear?'

He nodded.

'Nowhere else. Just home. Tell them that the police are here and that everything is all right. Just that.'

He nodded again.

'Nowhere else. Do I have to repeat that?'

'No, ma'am.'

'Cut across the fields. That should keep you out of sight from the house. Now hurry.'

'Yes, ma'am,' and he was halfway through the kitchen and then out the kitchen door. I noted that he opened the door carefully. I barely heard the *creak* of the half-rusted hinges.

There was no sound from upstairs to suggest that Allen had heard anything at all.

The flashes had stopped, or at least slowed, so he might be occupied looking around, poking in drawers and checking for . . . for whatever his imagination told him he would find to tie Carver to the death.

Because *that* was what he really wanted to do. I could tell by the look on his face and the sound of his voice that he wasn't particularly interested in the details, as long as he could pin the death on Carver.

'Victoria,' I began.

'Shhh.' She held her finger over her lips and then gestured toward the armchair.

I sat down but she wandered around the room for a few moments, touching this or that knick-knack, picking up a photograph from the highboy and studying it, then wandering over to the window and looking out.

I wanted to interrupt the silence, to ask any number of questions.

Who was Eric Johansson and how did he fit into the world of Fox Creek as I had come to know it? He seemed alien, a stranger, even lying in death. His clothing, what I had heard of his attitude.

Nothing really seemed to fit.

What was the relationship between Carver and Eric? If they were just casual neighbors, why was Carver the only one the other boy could ask for a ride when he was hurting and no doubt confused. Or worse.

Was it possible that Carver might have been involved in the beating? I knew that the boy had a bit of a temper, that he was apt to act on his emotions before he gave his reason a chance to intervene, but to beat another human being that savagely? I wasn't sure I could believe that.

But then, I had only known Carver — and Victoria, for that matter — since the early weeks of summer, so perhaps there was more to him than I understood.

I sat and waited.

The stale smell in the house seemed to grow stronger as the minutes passed, and every now and then I heard a bump or scrape from upstairs, as if Allen were shoving the furniture around.

Looking for something.

It might have been ten minutes — or perhaps twenty — when we heard the *clump* of his boots on the stairs.

A moment later, he was standing in front of Victoria, holding out a plastic bag about a quarter full of some white powder.

I could guess what it might be but I didn't want to.

'Found it,' he announced triumphantly, as if Victoria had challenged him to find it, or at least had argued that he never would.

'I'm so glad for you. Deputy Wroten will be proud.' I could hardly believe the sarcasm in her voice.

Apparently neither could Allen, because he all but visibly wilted. He thrust the bag into an inner pocket of his vest, muttering, 'Evidence,' and turned his back on Victoria.

He glanced at me and started to say something, then whirled to face Victoria again.

'Where's Ellis? *Ellis!*' he roared the latter, as if sheer volume would bring the boy out of whatever cubbyhole he had found to hide in.

'There's no need to yell,' Victoria said.

Her voice was more normal but there was still an edge to it that said that in spite of anything the officer might have found upstairs she still didn't appreciate his attitude toward her, me, or Carver. 'He's not here.'

Allen's hand went to his belt, where he started to yank at his radio.

'There's no need for that, either. He's just next door. I sent him over there to check on his mother and Mrs. Johansson.'

'You sent . . . ' I've rarely heard a grown man sputter, but Deputy Allen *sputtered*. 'You . . . What do you think gives you the right to . . . '

'The right to treat a boy who has just had a huge shock like a human being and not like some animal to be ordered around? Was that what you were going to say?'

'You had best take care, Mrs. Sears' — he purposely dropped the *Miz* that most people in Fox Creek used when talking to older women, whether married or not, and substituted the precise, legal term to indicate her wedded state, even though she had been a widow for longer than he had been alive — 'you best take care. You're talking to a duly appointed officer of the law, and . . . '

'And if you behaved like an objective observer instead of judge, jury, and hangman, I'd speak to you as one.'

He stared at her, his jaw dropping slightly.

'And in any case, you said nothing about him — or any of us — remaining in this house. None of us are under arrest, and unless you have found something upstairs to indicate otherwise, none of us will be.

'I assume that the packet you found contains drugs.'

Nonplussed, he answered in spite of himself. 'Yes, ma'am.'

Victoria could have that effect on people, I had discovered. Even people who didn't particularly like her.

'Young Eric's, I suppose. Pity. Pity.'

There was a long moment of silence. I think Deputy Allen was almost afraid to say anything.

Then he seemed to recover his aplomb. 'All right, you two follow me.'

Without checking to see if we were obeying his orders, he stalked into the kitchen and threw open the back door.

It squeaked hideously, as if to spite him. I think I saw him wince.

Victoria followed sedately, and I trailed after her.

'My vehicle,' Allen said curtly when we started toward my car.

Victoria stiffened again and I prepared myself for another confrontation. Then she apparently though better of what she was going to say and instead smiled sweetly and said, 'Oh, my! I've never ridden in a patrol car before,' making it sound as if Allen had politely invited her to take advantage of a once-in-a-lifetime-not-to-be-repeated invitation.

She walked over to the passenger door . . . and waited.

I didn't want to interrupt anything she had in mind, so I stood back for a moment and watched.

Deputy Allen stood frozen by the driver's door for a long moment, then said, rather icily, 'In the back seat, ma'am.'

'Oh, I don't think so. Isn't that where the criminals ride?'

He glared at her. By all rights she should have disintegrated on the spot and spiraled away in a tiny puff of dust.

Instead, she smiled even more sweetly.

'And doesn't the gentleman usually open the door for the lady?'

Actually, I wasn't sure whether to stare in disbelief at what she was doing or laugh my head off watching Deputy Allen trying to figure out what *he* would do.

What were his options, after all?

Arrest her for . . . well, for impudence unbecoming a senior citizen?

Order her to get in the back seat and then wonder what to do if she refused? I couldn't quite see him manhandling a little old woman, especially not with a witness standing only a few feet away.

Argue with her, and thereby lose even more face than he had already.

Or just give in to the inevitable.

He chose the latter. Sighing heavily and re-setting his uniform hat more firmly on his head, he stalked around the car, made a grand display of opening the front door and, bowing slightly at the waist, inviting his tiny seventy-plus-year-old adversary to take her seat.

He did, however, refrain from taking her arm to help her in.

She got in, settled herself, buckled up, and turned to look at him as if to say, 'Well, now that we have settled the question of who is in charge here, let's be off.'

All she said was, 'Thank you, officer.'

Even I couldn't hear the slightest hint of condescension in her voice.

I think that made him even angrier.

He stomped back to the driver's side and without a word to me got in behind the wheel.

Half-afraid that he would take off without me, I slid into the back seat, not bothering to make any comments about *my* not being a criminal.

I wasn't sure what Victoria was doing, but I was sure that she had something in mind. I knew that she wouldn't just bait Deputy Allen for the fun of it. She had better things to do with her time.

No, she was seriously worried about

something . . . perhaps Carver, and she wanted to be clear that she intended to be involved in whatever investigation was to follow.

I think things would have gone much more smoothly for the police if Deputy Wroten had been in the substation to take the call.

6

Allen peeled rubber backing out of the Johansson's drive, whipped around the corner onto the county road, the rear of his car heading speeding *away* from the Ellis' place, braked hard enough to rattle me in my seat, then laid rubber again as he jammed the gas pedal and the car leaped forward.

I'm surprised he didn't have the entire row of bubble-gum lights on the top of the car flashing and blinking.

Almost immediately, he had to brake again for the turn into the Ellis place. This time he threw me forward, against the protective webbing of my seat belt.

Gravel flew from his tires as he sped down the driveway and squealed to a halt next to the kitchen door.

Through it all, not a word, not a sound of surprise or complaint from Victoria.

But she did wait in her seat until Allen — who by that time was out of the car and halfway to the kitchen door, hand outstretched for the door knob — realized that she wasn't following, that she hadn't even exited the patrol car yet, and finally made his way around the front bumper to open the passenger door and bow her out.

'Why thank you, officer,' she said, as unruffled as if she had just arrived at the opening cotillion of the Season at some high-class ballroom in the big city.

He didn't answer.

Nor did he say anything until we entered the Ellises' living room.

Mrs. Ellis was seated on the couch, about where she had been earlier that morning. I assumed that Mrs. Johansson was resting in another room, since she was not present.

Carver was standing by the end of the sofa.

'Ellis!' Allen yelled. He was across the room in two long strides, had grabbed Carver by the shirt and slammed him against the closest wall before any of us could speak a word.

'What do you think you're trying to

pull?' Allen roared, although there was little chance that Carver could have answered him since the deputy now had one forearm tight against the boy's throat. 'What makes you think you can go wandering around the goddamn countryside in the middle of *my* investigation?'

He punctuated the question — clearly rhetorical — with another slam against the wall. Several pictures clattered in their frames but nothing fell.

'Deputy Allen,' Victoria began, but it was clear the man was paying no attention to her at all.

'Nobody leaves the scene of the crime until *I* give them permission! Do . . . you . . . under . . . stand . . . that!'

By this point, poor Carver's face was crimson with suffused blood and his eyes were beginning to bulge.

Victoria tried again: 'Deputy Allen! You must . . . '

'I've heard enough from you,' Allen called over his shoulder. His eyes were still focused on Carver's face. 'No more meddling in my . . . '

'Deputy Allen.' This time the voice was

quiet but firm, carrying throughout the room although no one had heard the speaker enter.

And it was masculine.

I looked over to see Deputy Richard Wroten, the officer in charge of the Fox Creek substation, standing in the doorway between the kitchen and the living room.

Allen froze for an instant, arm still half-choking Carver, then he dropped his arm and turned.

'Dick,' Allen said. His mouth kept on working, as if he wanted to say more but had no idea how to form the proper words or how to force them out.

'That's enough, Ewart,' Wroten said. 'You can let the young man go. I don't think he will be a flight risk . . . today.'

Allen dropped his arm. Carver bent over, hacking and coughing. His mother looked as if she wanted to rush to his side and comfort him but was afraid to move.

For a moment, things were rather tense.

'Now,' Wroten said, 'let's all sit down and figure out what is going on. Deputy Allen, you start.'

Allen dropped into a wooden-back chair by a small desk — probably where Janet Ellis sat once a month to make out checks for recurring bills — and explained what he had found at the Johansson house: the three of us standing over an obviously battered body, the bedroom in disarray, the small packet of what was probably cocaine, and coming downstairs to discover Carver missing.

'I thought he might have run off, you know, like before.'

'And *I* told you precisely where he had gone and why,' Victoria added.

'Right,' Wroten said, shifting to face her. 'Now, Miz Sears, what do you know about this?'

'Precious little, I'm afraid, Deputy Wroten.' I could hear in her voice that she placed a good deal more confidence in the older man than she did in his subordinate. 'Eric Johansson is dead. We left him where we found him . . . just *as* we found him, on the bed in his room.'

Wroten nodded. 'I've got a man over there now, watching the place.'

'Good. Well, we know that he was alive

late last night, when Carver brought him home from Land's End.'

'That right?' Wroten shot a glance at Carver, who seemed to have recovered somewhat from his near-strangulation.

Carver nodded.

'And we know that he had been beaten rather severely,' Victoria said. 'Twice. Once yesterday afternoon, and again late last night.'

Wroten's eyebrows shot up.

'Twice? By the same men?'

'No, I don't think so. And I think the . . . uh, the circumstances of the . . . two events were quite different. From what Carver told us, Eric got into a small fracas over at Tom Neilson's place late yesterday afternoon. Something to do with putting up grain.'

'That right?' Wroten seemed to be able to accomplish with a few words what Allen would probably never have managed.

Carver nodded. 'He and Mr. Neilson started to mix it up. I stepped in to try to calm Rick and he took a swing at me.' He glanced from Wroten to Victoria and

81

back, as if hoping for her support in what he was saying. 'But I didn't hit him, I didn't. Mr. Neilson clobbered Rick with a right-cross and Rick went down. That's all that happened.'

'Okay.'

'Then Rick took off. I guess to Land's End. I didn't hear any more from him until after midnight, when he called to say that Rafferty, that's the barkeep, Miz Hanson' — he added for my benefit — 'that Rafferty took his keys and wouldn't let him drive and he needed a ride. I drove over and picked him up. Whatever went on over there had already happened because he was bleeding and weaving back and forth like he had drunk up half the liquor in the bar.'

'So you don't know what went on at the bar?' Wroten asked.

Carver made as if to answer, but he never got the chance.

'I do. They killed him. They killed my baby's baby.' The voice came from the hallway entrance.

Greta Johansson.

'Greta,' Victoria said, surging to her

82

feet and crossing the room to offer the woman her arm. 'I thought you were resting.'

'How can I rest when my grandson is at my house, in his bed, dead. And *they killed him*. I know they did.'

Wroten was also on his feet, supporting Mrs. Johansson from the other side. Together he and Victoria got her to the sofa and helped her to sit down.

She still looked frail and shaky, but she seemed more herself than she had earlier. And she sounded a little better as well.

'Now, Miz Johansson, who do you think killed Eric?'

'I don't *think*, I *know!*' Her passion gave her voice a power it had lacked before. 'That bunch that hangs out at that . . . that *place*.'

She stopped, apparently convinced that she had said everything necessary.

It wasn't enough for Wroten.

'Do you mean the Land's End Bar, ma'am?'

She nodded mutely.

'And what *bunch*? Do you know any names?'

Again she nodded. It took her a moment or two to be able to speak.

'I don't know their real names. Eric never told me. He didn't talk about them much, but I would overhear things on the phone sometimes, when he was arranging to meet them. I know there was a Billy, and a Scooter. But the one he was afraid of was the leader. *Snake*.'

Wroten glanced at Allen, who nodded slightly. Apparently they knew who this mysterious 'Snake' was . . . and weren't happy about the knowledge.

'Now, ma'am, you say they killed your grandson?'

She nodded and began weeping into her handkerchief.

'Do you mean that they were the ones who beat him up last night?'

She shrugged. It was a pitiable gesture, full of hopelessness and resignation and despair.

'I don't know. They must have though.'

She fell silent. Wroten did not press for any more. He knew it would come when she was able to formulate her thoughts more clearly.

'When my Freddie died, and Rita — such a lovely woman and a perfect daughter-in-law — and poor Eric had nowhere else to turn, he came up here to live with me. I thought that it would be wonderful, him living here and all, someone to help out around the place. I'm not able to do all the things I used to, and he was young and strong and . . . oh, and such a *good* little boy. He used to visit when he was just a boy and we would sit for hours and talk and tell stories and play games. He loved it.

'I thought it would be the same now.

'But it wasn't. When he arrived, his hair was all spiky and he had . . . *things* . . . in his ears and his eyebrows, and his clothes were all tattered and torn, even though I knew that Freddie and Rita made enough to give him new clothes any time he wanted them.

'And he was . . . different. He was moody and sullen and sometimes we would go days on end and he wouldn't even talk to me. He would just sit in his room, hours on end. I'd ask him what he was doing and he would say, 'Just thinkin', Grams, just thinkin'.'

'Finally, I told him that he would have to start helping out more. If he didn't want to do things here at the place, he could at least find work. And he did, now and again. Like yesterday, when he went to the Neilson place. He'd done that before.

'But he also started going out at night.

'He wouldn't tell me where, but like I said, I heard things sometimes when he talked on the telephone. He would take my old car and not come home until way late, and I knew that he was going out to that place on the State highway, you know, just out of town.

'He would drink and smoke. I could smell that on him the next day. And he started talking back to me and being . . . '

She began weeping again. Victoria repeated her 'There, there' gesture for a few minutes. Finally Mrs. Johansson looked up, directly into Wroten's eyes.

'I don't know what-all he got up to out at that place. But after he started going there, there wasn't anything left of my little grandbaby any more. I had a stranger living in my house, eating my food.

'Whatever . . . *whoever* killed him, it was out at that God-forsaken place. *They killed him. They killed my baby's baby!*'

7

Deputy Wroten's second priority was to view the body.

First, he spent nearly half an hour sequestered with Deputy Allen in Janet Ellis's kitchen, just out of earshot, reviewing Allen's notes, his observations and conclusions. Then, after instructing Allen to remain at the Ellis's with Janet and Mrs. Johansson, he told Victoria, Carver, and me to meet him at the Johansson house.

'Directly there, mind you,' he added, as if throwing a bone to Allen, who looked as if he had been thoroughly reprimanded for his attitude toward and his earlier actions against Carver.

As if there was anywhere else we were likely to go.

The additional thirty or forty minutes he spent in Eric Johansson's bedroom — closely watched by Victoria and, I must admit, somewhat less closely by me, with

Carver waiting just outside the door — were in large part a repeat of what we had seen earlier that morning.

The body was unmoved, in spite of the rattling and banging we had heard while Allen had examined the room. One drawer was fully open and its contents clearly disturbed — that was most likely where he had discovered the hidden packet of drugs.

The major difference was that, since Wroten knew that Allen had photographed the body and the rest of the room, he showed no compunctions about pulling the T-shirt, now caked and stiff and rusty-red, up far enough for us all to see that the bruises, scrapes, and other wounds extended nearly to the throat.

Whoever had beaten Eric Johansson had obviously been furious about something.

'Are those stab wounds.' Victoria asked at one point, indicating several long, narrow patches of dried blood along the rib cage.

Wroten leaned further over to inspect them.

'Not sure. Could be. If they are, they're awfully shallow to have been the cause of death. We'll know more when Doc Anderson has a chance to look at them.'

'Where is Doctor Anderson?' I asked, suddenly aware that the coroner had been absent all morning.

'He and most of his staff are at a training session down-mountain,' Wroten said. 'It's only one day, and he figured whatever came up could wait a while.'

He shook his head and studied the wounds again.

'Guess he figured wrong. The best we can do is put the body on ice and wait until tomorrow . . . or the next day for the answers to some of our questions.'

'Then someone is coming to take care of . . . ' Victoria trailed off.

'Yes, ma'am. The coroner's van should be here in an hour or so. It's been busy with another death — this one long-anticipated and well-documented, over at the old folks' home in Six Pines.'

That was the closest town to Fox Creek, about twenty-five miles further down the State Highway.

'Old Mrs. Weimer?' Victoria looked saddened but not shocked.

'Yes, ma'am. She'd been fading for a couple of weeks, and we got the call at about five this morning.'

'Well,' Victoria said, 'she was well along. Had to have been nearly ninety. Poor old thing. No family, not many friends left alive. She must have been terribly lonely. I should have visited her more often.'

'The funeral will be here in Fox Creek, then?'

'Yes, ma'am. A couple of grandchildren from down-mountain will be coming in sometime this afternoon or tomorrow.'

'So sad.'

And then they turned their attention back to young Eric Johansson, who would never know the loneliness of outliving those closest to him, or feel the disappointment of grandchildren who remained distant . . . or uncaring.

'What about his thighs?' Victoria made as if to lift the torn edge of the jeans.

'I'd better do that, Miz Sears,' Wroten said, and he carefully peeled the torn flap of denim up toward the waistband, revealing even more evidence of beating and kicking.

'Must've gotten to him when he was on the ground. He'd have curled up to protect himself, and that would account for all of the bruises along the outside there.'

'Hmmm, yes,' Victoria said, but she wasn't exactly looking at the thigh. She was concentrating on the upper surface of the leg, just at the knee cap and extending for a few inches above.

The skin was torn, shredded almost, raw and ragged. She leaned over so close that it looked as if she might be about to smell the wounds, but then she straightened up and half-nodded to herself.

Wroten apparently didn't catch the small gesture.

I did but I didn't dare ask Victoria about it yet. It looked as if she had had a thought but that it had passed almost as quickly as it came. When she glanced over at me, her eyes were calm, sad, retrospective.

'I guess that's all we can do here,'

Wroten said finally. 'Next stop should probably be Land's End.'

'I think, if you don't mind, that it might be instructive to drop by the Neilson farm first. To get more of a chronological sense of yesterday, as it were. And it's really just on the way, about halfway to Land's End.'

Now it was Wroten's turn to look as if he wanted to ask a question but didn't quite dare. He studied Victoria for a long moment, then nodded and said, 'Don't see any harm in that.'

Downstairs, he instructed Carver, Victoria, and me — the designated driver — to follow him, and we set out for the Neilson farm. At least there was no discussion over who might or might not have to sit in the 'criminal' seat in his vehicle.

It took about twenty minutes to get to the Neilson place. Normally, I would have been trying to get as much information as I could out of Victoria, but she sat stolidly in the passenger seat, not particularly withdrawn, but watching the fields as they flickered past. She surely had something on her mind, but I decided she was still working on making sense out of it. I didn't want to interrupt her.

Carver was in the back seat, taciturn and unspeaking. I know he would have felt humiliated at the way Allen had treated him in front of the rest of us, including his mother — I know I would have felt that way — and didn't want to talk to anyone right then. I didn't even try.

Instead, I concentrated on the road, on the back bumper of Deputy Wroten's cruiser, on the light glinting off his taillights, on the fact that it was probably getting on to ten or eleven o'clock and I hadn't had anything to eat except a bagel and a glass of milk.

The Neilson place was newer, more modern-looking, better kept up than either the Ellises' or the Johanssons'. The rail fence was newly painted, the roof of the two story brick house newly shingled. Everything looked bright and shiny and polished.

We waited in the car while Deputy Wroten spoke to an elderly woman — Mrs. Neilson, perhaps? — who couldn't seem to speak three words in a row without using her hands to wave and point. After a couple of minutes, Wroten approached the car. I rolled the window down.

'Tom Neilson's in the field today, same one where the Johansson kid was working yesterday. I just got a knock-down-and-drag-out second-hand version of things from Tom's mother back there' — the woman was still standing at the kitchen door, arms folded, looking like she could face down hordes of ravening Nazis if they tried to accuse her beloved son of anything — 'then she said he was out there trying to get the flatbed back into working condition.

'It's not far. Just follow me and keep close.'

It wasn't far. It took perhaps ten minutes on graveled roads, turning left and right where fields ended and, presumably, other farmers' fields began.

We saw Neilson and a couple of hands long before they saw us. They were grouped around a flatbed that was canted partway in an irrigation ditch, its load of neatly stacked bales holding on as firmly as if it had been dead-level. Nearby was a pickup truck, a combine, and a baler, all standing silent and empty. The field looked as if it had been about three-quarters finished before something had gone wrong with the flatbed.

Wroten got out first, spoke a few words to a man a couple of years older than me, who seemed to answer easily and without any signs of anger, then he signaled for us to join him.

'Miz Sears, you know Tom, of course.'

'Of course. His parents and I go back a long way. Good to see you, Tom.' She extended her hand.

The man removed his worn leather work glove, took her proffered hand, and shook it firmly.

'And you know Carver, I guess, since he was working out here yesterday.'

A nod passed between the two men. No need for a handshake right then.

'And this pretty lady' — had he actually *said* that? — 'is Lynn Hanson. She's staying the summer at the Van Etten's place, up by Miz Sears's.'

The man — Tom Neilson apparently

— nodded and extended his hand. In spite of having probably been encased in the leather glove all morning, his hand was dry and warm, and his fingers felt strong and capable as they grasped mine. He could easily have crushed my knuckles, I realized, but he didn't even pretend to try.

It was very much a gentleman's handshake. I liked it.

I decided at the same time that I would probably like Mr. Neilson as well.

Wroten was already asking questions. Apparently he had not yet told Neilson — or the other hands who had clustered close by — that Johansson was dead. He was treating it like he just wanted some background on the boy. Maybe the kid had been speeding, or spraying graffiti on a wall somewhere in town. Something relatively minor but that needed to be dealt with.

Neilson answered his questions clearly and directly, without any apparent hesitation. His story matched Carver's.

The Johansson kid had been hired as day labor and had spent most of the afternoon on the flatbed boosting and stacking the bales as they were handed up by the rest of the crew. He did an all right job, Neilson said, until about two hours before quitting time.

Then he had complained about feeling a bit feverish and achy.

'Not used to so much *man*-u-al labor, that kid,' one of the hands said. He was an older man, probably in his fifties, and looked as if he had spent every day of those years out in the field.

'That's enough, Ed. He did a good enough job. Enough to earn the wage I was paying.'

The kid figured that he would do better driving the truck than wrestling the heavy bales, and the driver — another of the regular hands, named Bill — had no objections, so he had handed over the driver's seat to the kid . . . who promptly drove the rig into the irrigation ditch.

That would have been bad enough, since it would have taken valuable time to pull it out. But the kid had somehow managed to mangle the front axle and, for the time being, the flatbed would be out of commission.

'It was hot, we'd been working all day, and I'll admit it, I lost my temper. The thing with the flatbed was a stupid mistake that shouldn't have happened. But then he tried to weasel out of being responsible for the truck, whining about how bad he felt, and I lost it. I came at him, he started toward me, Carver there stepped in between and got sucker-punched by the kid, and I let the kid have it.

'He went down, I fired him on the spot and told him to pick up his pay on the way out, and he got up, dusted off his sorry ass, and stomped away.

'End of fight. End of story.

'Except that he forgot to go by the house and get his pay. I guess I'll have to mail it to him.'

'That'll take some mighty fancy postage,' Wroten said.

'What?'

'Eric Johansson is dead.'

'Dead?'

'Sometime last night.'

'How . . . ? Was it a car accident? Or . . . ?'

'So far all we know is that he was

beaten up pretty badly. Head, face, torso, even kicked all to hell along the legs. Somebody, or somebodies did a full-out work-over on him.'

'Hey,' Neilson said, starting to take a step back, then stopping and standing his ground, 'you don't think I had anything to do with that? I gave him a good one, I told you that already, but he walked away from it and I haven't seen him since.'

'Care to tell me where you were last night?'

'Sure. I was here until nightfall, along with the rest of the boys, working on this pile of scrap metal — that's pretty much what it's worth unless I can fix it. Then we all went back to the house and had a long, well-deserved dinner. Mom and I stayed up until, oh, maybe twelve-thirty, one o'clock, watching a little T.V. and trying to figure out how we were going to get the rest of the wheat harvested without that damn . . . without the flatbed. Then I went to bed.

'I didn't see Johansson again after he left this field. I swear to it.'

I believed him. Not that that meant

anything, of course, but there was something about him that rang true.

I think Wroten felt the same, because he gave up questioning Neilson, satisfied just to warn him to stay close in case anything else came up. Standard stuff. I'd heard it before, actually.

Just after the accident that had killed Terry and Shawn.

Funny, I could think that sentence and not get the shakes.

I looked around for Victoria. I half expected to see her standing near Deputy Wroten, taking in all of the questions and answers. Instead, she was walking around the flatbed, staring up at the bales of hay, checking out something on the ground a few feet from the truck, or standing and simply staring into space, thinking.

'Victoria,' I called.

She glanced over at me, gave me a little wave, and made her way back to the group.

'Are you finished here, Richard?'

'Yes, ma'am. And are you?'

'I think so. However, I think it might be . . . uh, wisdom if you were to request that Tom not move any of this equipment, not even to repair the flatbed, for a day or so, at least not until Doc Anderson has had a chance to examine the body. Would that be possible, Tom?'

Evidently she had taken Wroten's agreement for granted, since she was looking directly at Neilson when she finished.

'I . . . well, I suppose so. I was going to off-load the bales to another flatbed if I could borrow one, maybe from Mitch Knowles or Evan Sanders . . .'

'I think that might be unwise,' Victoria said softly. 'Don't you agree, Deputy?'

'Yeah, okay. It is a death from unknown causes. Better be safe than sorry, right, Tom?'

Neilson nodded.

'Well, then, Richard,' Victoria said lightly. 'Shall we go on to Land's End.'

'After me, ma'am.' Wroten made a small gesture, as if he were about to doff his hat to her.

They both smiled. It wasn't the time or the place for an outright laugh.

8

Land's End Bar was an unprepossessing building, long and narrow and low-seeming, painted a rusty green. It had a single entrance visible from the State Highway and a pair of long and narrow windows high up in the walls on each side of the door. It was shaded by plane trees that were, from their girth, substantially older than the building, even though the bar itself looked well advanced in years.

'Land's End?' I asked, addressing myself to no one in particular. The four of us — Deputy Wroten, Victoria, Carver, and I — were standing in the roughly paved parking lot. At the far end of the lot, nearly on the other side of the building, half a dozen dust-grimed pickups were parked in a rough row, looking like horses in an old-time Western tethered outside the saloon, waiting patiently for their riders. Carver pointed out one of them as Mrs. Johansson's. To all appearances it had not been moved since the afternoon before.

'No idea,' Wroten said. 'It's been called that for as long as I can remember. Sounds like it should be out on a headland somewhere, looking out to sea. It's been through several changes of ownership over the years but the name always remains the same.'

'I can see why owners might want to sell out,' I commented. 'It doesn't look exactly prosperous.'

'It's looked just like this for as long as I can remember, too. Run-down, beat-up, sagging along the roofline. But there's a fair crowd out here on the week-ends. It's outside the city limits, you see, so it's exempt from some of the rather Draconian laws the City Council imposes on licensed liquor establishments.'

'I don't believe I've ever been this close to it,' Victoria said. 'I've driven past, of course, but usually it just passes through my vision, part of the landscape to be ignored and forgotten.'

'I can't say that my experiences with the place have been quite that neutral. We get fairly frequent calls for d-and-d — that's *drunk and disorderly* to the layperson,' Wroten said, addressing himself to me.

'I've heard the term. Believe it or not, we actually have bars in the big city, too,' I answered. He grinned at me, catching my light sarcasm. Deputy Allen would probably have tried to cuff me for insubordination, insolence, or something else.

'Well, we may as well see what we can learn,' Victoria said.

'Are you sure you want me to come in with you?' Carver sounded a bit uncertain. 'I didn't actually go in last night. I picked Rick up here in the parking lot.'

'Where?'

'Over there,' he said, pointing to a stretch of packed dirt along the side of the building.

Wroten walked over, searching the ground. At one point he knelt and followed something with his fingertip, as if he had found a track. He waved Victoria over. I followed, but Carver remained where he was standing.

'Here,' Wroten said, indicating some dark brown splotches. 'Blood, I think. Certainly signs of a scuffle. One of the guys was down.' He pointed to a long series of curving lines where the dirt looked like it had been swept. 'That would probably be Johansson. There were two, maybe three others. The ground's too hard to be sure. But I'd guess that whatever happened . . . or at least the last round of whatever happened, happened out here.'

He stood, backed away a bit, and squatted down to take a few photographs.

'Where was Johansson waiting when you got here?'

Carver took a few steps closer to where the rest of us were standing.

'Right there, leaning against the wall.'

'How bad did he look?'

'Well, it was pretty dark. The lights don't hit much of the parking lot. He looked like he was hurt. I could see blood on his face, and he was hunched over a little, like he was holding his gut.'

'Probably a few broken ribs, judging from the bruises I saw,' Wroten said. His face looked grim. 'Why didn't you take him to the hospital?'

'He wanted to go home. Said he'd be all right. He sounded drunk, you know, slurring and hard to understand. He was pretty wobbly but made it into my car on his own power and he didn't start really fading until we were at his place. He was still awake when I wrestled him upstairs, otherwise we'd have never made it.'

'Looks like he might have thrown up here,' Wroten said. 'Wouldn't be surprised, if he was that drunk. Must have hurt like a bitch with all those scrapes and bruises.'

'Yes, well, should we go on in now?' Victoria began moving toward the front door.

'You sure you want to go in with me?'

'I don't *want* to, but we really have to try to figure this out, don't we.'

'Yes, ma'am. *We* do.'

The inside of Land's End was, to begin with, *dark*.

For a moment, I felt as if I had been blinded.

It took several minutes for our eyes to

get accustomed to the intentional twilight everywhere, except over the bar.

It was a fair sized room, with a row of booths along one wall, small square tables surrounded by chairs scattered along the center, and the bar at the far end. A man stood behind the bar, working on something. He ignored us as we came in.

I thought that peculiar.

Unless he was expecting some kind of fallout from the events of the night before and knew that we were the ones bringing it. The idea didn't comfort me at all.

There were a couple of mirrors behind the bar, some plate-glass shelving holding bottles of various colored liquids. I'm not a connoisseur of adult beverages, so I couldn't identify any of them by sight. I doubt I could have identified more than a few by taste.

An old-fashioned jukebox shared the long wall with a door, currently closed, that presumably led to another room.

Even though it was clearly long before opening time, there were several people there, the most visible being a couple of old men who no doubt made Land's End home-away-from-home for most of the daytime hours and a goodly portion of the night. I wouldn't be surprised to find out that the bartender opened the place especially for them, just so they would have somewhere to go during the day.

Mostly the place was silent. I thought I heard a soft clicking sound from the direction of the other room. And maybe, occasionally, men's voices whispering. There was probably a pool table in there. I wondered who would be using it in the middle of the day.

The old men, I could understand. Pool hustlers were a different story.

The man behind the bar finally deigned to glance up and acknowledge our presence.

'Deputy.'

'Rafferty.'

It was clear that the two men had done business before from the tones of their voices, the slight movements of their heads that comprised recognition, greetings, and — on Rafferty's part at least — wariness. As soon as Wroten had uttered his name, the other man lowered his gaze back toward the bar.

'Help you?' Rafferty was doing something behind the long, shiny bar that stretched along the entire end of the room. Whatever it was, it required a pad of paper, a stubby pencil, a pile of loose papers of assorted sizes, and absolutely all of his attention. Other than raising his head for that phantom greeting when Wroten had first entered, he had not moved.

Wroten stepped across the room toward the bar.

It was not quite the John-Wayne, thumbs-in-the-belt, boot-heels-slicking-on-the-hardwood-floor, I-don't-give-a-shit-who-you-are-or-what-you-think-because-*I*-am-the-law swagger familiar from hundreds of bad movies and mediocre television shows but it wasn't far from it either.

Yes, there had been business between these two before, not always pleasant, and Deputy Wroten was performing in the persona that the situation required. I didn't know him all that well, but I had seen him at work before, when this kind of braggadocio had not been needed.

I liked him better the other way.

Still, the act did its job. As soon as Wroten crossed a certain invisible line across the floor, the other man carefully placed his pencil cross-wise on the pad, placed both hands ostentatiously — and fully visibly — onto the bar and leaned forward slightly. His version of 'Okay, you're the law, all right. What do you want?'

'Heard there was a bit of trouble out here last night. Care to tell me about it?'

'You mean with that punk city kid? Spiky hair? Ripped up clothes?'

'That's the one. Kid got a name?' I suppose he was trying to find out, without actually asking, if Eric Johansson had frequented Land's End.

'Yeah, that Johansson kid.'

Okay, so he had.

'His name was Eric, sir,' Carver said from the darkness behind me. His voice was tight and strained and made him sound like he was about twelve years old.

Rafferty must have caught the adolescent pitch in it as well as I had.

'Who's that?' he called.

Carver stepped past me until he was only an arm's length behind Wroten.

111

'Hey, who are you?' Rafferty sounded honestly surprised. So he didn't recognize Carver.

'I'm Carver Ellis. I helped re-shingle your roof last spring.'

'Yeah, that's right. Now I . . . Hey, you're not old enough to be inside here, the age limit's posted right there on the front door. Deputy . . . '

He turned his attention to Wroten as if the officer was planning on arresting him for serving to a minor.

I must admit to a certain sense of relief. If Rafferty couldn't immediately place Carver's face, then the boy hadn't been in the bar before . . . or at least not often. I didn't want to think of Carver as drinking in a place like this. In fact, I couldn't imagine him drinking at all. It just didn't fit my image of him. So far my image was holding up fairly well, in spite of Deputy Allen's apparent assumption that in his spare time Carver was a wild-eyed homicidal maniac intent on single-handedly controlling the population explosion in Fox Creek.

Wroten made a quick gesture with one

hand, a kind of hold-the-horses-there flick of one hand.

'No one's accusing you of anything, Rafferty. Mr. Ellis here is with me. This is an official visit, not a social one.'

'Who else is there?'

Rafferty kind of squinted at us. Apparently the lights over the bar — unusually bright right now, no doubt to help him with whatever paperwork he was doing — made it hard for him to see the rest of the room. During regular business hours, the lighting would be more evenly distributed.

'Hello, Mr. Rafferty,' Victoria said, a bit primly perhaps but perfectly politely. 'I haven't seen you since the last Community Picnic. It's good to see you again.'

'Miz Sears?' Rafferty sounded taken aback. 'What are you doing in a . . . here.'

'Oh,' she laughed lightly, 'I'm part of an official police investigation. Isn't that exciting?'

I stared at her. First Wroten and his big-bad sheriff pose, now Victoria doing a Helen-Hayes little-ole-me bit.

I decided just to be me.

113

'I'm Lynn Hanson. I'm renting the Van Etten Place,' I said as evenly as possible.

'Ma'am.'

Formal greetings had been exchanged. Now it was up to Wroten.

I was a little surprised when he didn't repeat his request for Rafferty to talk about the events of the night before.

The silence lengthened. After a long few moments, Rafferty cleared his throat.

'All right. There was a . . . a set-to here last night. Young Johansson and a couple of locals.'

Eric Johansson had been living — permanently, from what I could gather — with his grandmother for the better part of a year. But he wasn't local. He probably would never be considered a local, even if he combed his hair just like everyone else, bought his clothes at the same stores, and spent hours with an elocutionist learning just the right touch of a drawl to help him blend in with everyone else.

Or he wouldn't have if he was still alive.

I expected Wroten to ask who else had been involved.

'What went on?'

'Not much. The Johansson kid . . . Rick came in half-soused. He was blinking like the light in here hurt his eyes, kind of weaving and stumbling, you know, not falling-down-drunk, not quite, but pretty far along the road.'

'You serve him anything more?'

'Nah. He never asked for anything. Just fumbled his way to one of the booths back there and half-collapsed in it. Normally I'd have insisted that he buy at least a beer, pretend to nurse it for a while, but like I said, he was pretty well out of it.

'I'd heard a car drive up just before he staggered in, so I figured I'd let him rest a bit — him being a fairly regular customer and all — and just be sure to get his keys before he tried to leave.

'I did, too.' Rafferty was almost bursting with glowing self-righteousness, the conscientious barkeep always on the lookout for the well-being of his clients. After serving them poison.

'You can ask the ki . . . Carver, there. I heard Johansson calling him for a ride because I took his keys.'

'Very civic-minded of you, I'm sure, Mr. Rafferty,' Victoria said. I could tell she felt the same way about the situation as I did.

'All right, Rafferty. We have Mr. Johansson sitting in the booth back there by himself. Then what?'

'For a while I would think he'd drifted off, then he'd shift around a bit. Once he got up to hit the head. But mostly he just sat there, staring.

'Then, maybe half an hour, three-quarters of an hour, a bunch of locals came in, like I said . . . '

Again a distinct hesitation about naming names. I began to wonder about that. And apparently Deputy Wroten did also, because instead of pressing that issue, he again skirted it, as if he wanted to see how long it would take Rafferty to cough up the information Wroten already knew . . . that it was the man Greta called 'Snake' who had entered.

'They . . . uh . . . they milled around the bar for a while, ordering beers, shooting the shi . . . shooting the breeze with a couple of guys sitting on the stools,

116

generally acting the way guys act when they stop in here after work, relaxing, letting off a little steam. Mostly laughing and arm-punching over jokes, that kind of thing.'

He paused and looked down at the pad and pencil with a kind of longing in his eyes, as if he would rather be doing the paperwork — as if he would rather be doing almost *anything* — that recounting what had happened to Eric Johansson.

'Then . . . I don't remember how it happened, but then they caught sight of the Johansson kid sitting back there in the dark, and they kind of drifted over that way. Not mean-like, not like they were aiming to start any trouble.

'At first, they just talked to him. I couldn't hear what they were saying, not over the noise in the rest of the room, so they must have been speaking pretty normal to him.'

'But he wasn't paying them any attention, was he.' Victoria said. It wasn't a question. It was a statement.

Her voice startled me. The little-old-lady pitch was gone and she sounded more like herself, clear-headed, sharp, insightful.

More than that, what she said startled me. And it startled Rafferty as well because he stopped speaking altogether and just stared at her.

'Well?' Wroten asked. 'Does Miz Sears have it right?'

'Uh . . . yeah. One of the guys grabbed Johansson by the shirt and pulled him out of the booth.

''Hey!' I yelled, and one of them turned to me and said, 'It's okay Rafferty, we're just talking to Spike here' — that's what they called him sometimes, Spike — 'and we want to make sure that he listens closely.''

''Yeah,' someone else said, ''cause paying close attention could be good for his health.''

'In other words,' Wroten said drily, 'several of your customers were manhandling and threatening another of your customers, who had already had too much to drink and was not fully aware of what was going on around him, and you stood back and did nothing.'

'Uh . . . it wasn't like that . . . uh . . . I

118

. . . he . . . ' Rafferty stumbled to a stop.

I wondered just how much Wroten knew about what went on in a place like Land's End.

Given the little scenarios Rafferty had just sketched, and the packet of white powder Allen had no doubt passed on to Wroten during their exchange of information in the kitchen, I was fairly sure that more than state-approved liquors changed hands in the Land's End.

'What happened then, Mr. Rafferty?' Victoria said quietly.

'Then?' Rafferty seemed almost to snap out of a trance. 'Yeah, then. Well, two of them grabbed Johansson under the arms and kind of walked him to the door. He didn't seem to mind.'

'I'm sure he didn't,' Victoria said softly.

'They stopped at the door and said they were taking him out for a breath of fresh air. And then they went out.'

'The whole group?' That was Wroten's voice.

'Uh . . . yeah. Five or six of them.'

'And did you hear anything else while the five or six of them were giving your

drunk customer a breath of fresh air?'
Wroten's contempt was clearly evident.

'No, I didn't,' Rafferty said firmly. 'Not
a sound. Not a thing. It's pretty quiet in
here and . . . '

At that moment an eighteen-wheeler
ripped past on the State Highway. We all
heard it clearly.

'It's . . . uh . . . pretty quiet in here,'
Rafferty continued, patently rattled but
giving it a good try nonetheless. 'I didn't
hear anything, I swear, Deputy.'

'Okay. What happened then? Did the
gang . . . ?'

'Hey,' Rafferty said, again the self-
righteous barkeep-slash-public servant, 'it
wasn't a gang. I don't allow gangs in my
place. They were just some . . . uh, guys
that stop by now and again.'

'Like every night?'

Rafferty didn't answer.

'So back to the 'five or six guys.' Did
they come back in?'

'No. They left after ten or fifteen
minutes. I heard their cars . . . No. They
didn't come back in.'

'And Mr. Johansson?'

At that, Rafferty had the good grace at least to look down at the bar. He couldn't meet Wroten's eyes.

'Yeah, he did. About half an hour later. He was . . . it looked like he was drunker than before, I don't know, like they had all shared some beer or something outside.'

Even I could tell that Rafferty didn't believe that pretty little story.

'And it looked like he must have . . . uh . . . fallen down in the parking lot or something. Like he hit his head. Maybe hurt his leg, because he was limping and kind of wincing now and again.'

'And out of the kindness of your heart, you asked him for his keys because he was too drunk to drive, let him use your telephone to call a friend, and then told him to wait *outside* until the friend could arrive.'

Again, not a question but a flat statement. Wroten was as good at that technique as Victoria was. There was no sign of the posturing, swaggering law-man now. Just a good — even outstanding — officer of the law zeroing in on a wrong-doer who had condemned himself by his own words.

'Look, Wroten, I didn't want any trouble in here. Outside is outside, you know. I didn't see anything and I didn't . . . '

'I know, you didn't hear anything.' Rafferty nodded.

'But you did hear something, didn't you, Mr. Rafferty,' Victoria said, again so quietly that you could hardly expect anyone else to hear. But we all did.

Rafferty did not answer. He held stiffly still, as if any movement might give him away. More than his words already had.

'Okay, Rafferty, just a couple more questions.'

Rafferty looked up at Wroten with a touch of wonder in his eyes, as if he could hardly believe that the rough part was over with so little damage done.

'Sure, anything.'

'You've told us pretty much everything that happened to Mr. Johansson while he was here, directly or indirectly, but you seem to have left out the most interesting part.'

'I did? What would that be?'

'Just the names of the 'five or six guys' that were so concerned for Johansson's health last night. Names that I'm pretty certain you know.'

'I . . . uh . . . no, I . . . '

Again, he stuttered to a halt.

'Come on, Rafferty. You know the names. Who was so interested in Eric Johansson last night?'

'That would be me,' said a calm, level voice from behind us.

9

I suddenly became aware of a silence in Land's End, a stillness that had not been there when we had entered.

The old fellows at the far table had stopped talking and were looking our way, but that wasn't what made the difference. They'd probably been watching us since we came in. Certainly beat the daytime entertainment on television. If there'd been a television handy.

No, this silence went deeper.

After a moment I recognized what had changed.

The subtle *click-click-click* had stopped, as had the susurrant undercurrent of men's voices from the other room, the one beyond the closed door.

Whoever had been playing pool had stopped sometime during our interchange.

And the door was open.

A young man stood in the doorway.

'Why, you must be Mr. Snake,' Victoria said into the silence, her little-old-lady intonations back in full play.

Even if we hadn't heard the nickname from Greta Johansson — even as she had been accusing him of murdering her grandson — 'Snake' would have been a likely enough guess.

He was perhaps my age, and tall, easily the tallest person in the bar, and wiry-thin. He had dirty-blond hair that stood straight up in a short, no-doubt fashionable cut, and a fringe of equally dirty-blond beard on his chin. He had high cheekbones and a strong, sensitive mouth.

But his eyes!

His eyes were a crystalline blue, lighter than sky-blue, almost as light as the glacial blue you sometimes see in pictures in the *National Geographic*.

Terry and Shawn and I had once vacationed in an old mining town in Arizona, and walking down the main street we had seen a huge cluster of crystals, easily five feet long and a foot high, on display in a jeweler's window. We had to go in and find out what it was.

The man behind the counter called it 'Bisbee Ice,' after the name of the little town. He said it was a gem-quality calcite only found in a single mine, long since played out, on the outskirts of the town.

I fell in love with the stone. The color was so cool, so clear, so deep, that I had to have a piece.

Terry ended up buying me 100 carats in half a dozen cut and polished cabochons . . . and spending over $200 dollars to do it, a healthy hunk of our spending money for the trip.

Later, he had them set in sterling silver as a pendant necklace and matching earrings. I still had three teardrop cabochons in my jewel case, folded into a bit of tissue paper and tucked into a small compartment. Someday, perhaps when the memory of that visit — the last one we took as a family — is less painful, I will have them set as well.

The image of Terry and Shawn *ooh*-ing and *ahh*-ing over the tray of cut stones as they tried to pick out the perfect ones for me hurt . . . not as deeply as it would have before I came up here to Fox Creek, I realized with a flood of relief, but it still hurt.

Even so, I loved the stones.

I loved their color.

And here was the same color, looking out at me from eyes that seemed as cold, as deep, as uncaring and as cruel as a glacier.

Eyes belonging to a man who had a discomfortingly real image of a rattle-snake on his right arm, tail coiled over his muscular shoulder, fully revealed in a white muscle shirt; body tattooed around the length of the arm, seeming to slither and twist with every movement; head — fangs fully extended and so life-like that I could almost see the venom oozing from their tips — a triangular monstrosity on the back of his hand.

I imagined that if the hand were clenched into a fist, and that fist were flying through the air at me, it would be as terrifying, as menacing, as a striking snake.

I shivered.

The man — *Snake* — glanced at

Victoria, studied her for a moment with his head cocked to one side, then made a mock bow.

'Gracious,' she said in response, 'What a polite young man.'

'Right,' Wroten said. His voice sounded rough in comparison. 'And the young man has a name, I believe. We've met before, once or twice.'

'That we have, Deputy, that we have,' the man said, totally unflustered. He angled his head back toward Victoria. 'Edward Garton, ma'am.' Again, he made the mock bow. I could almost hear him laughing behind his smile.

'Oh yes,' Victoria said — *gushed* actually — 'Little Eddie Garton. Why, I used to know your mother and father well, although I haven't had a chance to visit with Myra and Nathan in . . . well, in far too long. You know how it is with us old folks, it gets harder and harder to get out.'

At the words 'Little Eddie,' the man's eyes, already cold, immediately dropped a dozen degrees more, to well into the sub-zero range.

Victoria, I thought, *what are you doing? If this is the man who beat Eric so severely, he's too dangerous to toy with.*

Her next words frightened me even more . . . for her.

'I should have recognized you of course, but the last time I saw you — why, I believe it was at another Community Picnic on the 4th of July, over in Central Park, maybe fifteen years ago — you were nowhere near so tall. Or quite so . . . ah, stylishly ornamented.'

His hand jerked convulsively, as if he were about to make a fist. The rattlesnake coiled to strike.

Wroten stepped in, apparently sensing that Victoria was taking entirely the wrong tack with his suspect.

'Mr. Garton, I'd like to ask a couple of questions about last night.'

Garton sauntered over to one of the tables and dropped down into a chair. Behind him, three or four men, a few years younger than he, clustered by the door, lounging back against the wall.

But I could tell that, like their master, they were also coiled and ready to strike.

'I'd ask you to call me 'Snake,' like all my *friends* do, Deputy Wroten, but I don't think you would. Anyway, what do you want to know?'

'We've been talking to Rafferty here about some unpleasantness last night. Between you and Eric Johansson.'

'That would be 'Spike,'' Garton — Snake — said complacently. 'We all have names that fit our personalities. I'd introduce you to the rest of the . . . to the rest of my friends, but I sense that you're not really interested in their names right now.'

'I'll get to that later. Right now, I'd like to hear your version of what happened.'

'But Deputy Wroten, there is no *version* of it. There is only the *truth*. Truth is truth. There can't be versions of the truth, can there?'

He was playing Wroten masterfully, skimming on the near edge of insult and non-cooperation but adroitly avoiding crossing any lines.

I glanced around to see where Carver was. He had backed away from us when Snake had entered the room and was now perched on a stool by the bar.

Good. Keep him out of the worst danger.

Victoria, on the other hand, had moved closer to Snake and — to my utter horror — taken a seat at the side of the same table, where she proceeded to watch him with a frightening intensity.

I hoped she was just trying to unnerve him with her presence.

'All right, Garton. Tell us the *truth* then.'

'Well,' Garton said, leaning back in his chair and crossing his legs at the ankles, revealing heavy, highly polished boots with steel caps on the toes. 'Me and a few of my friends came by last night, you know, for a bit of R & R after a hard day at the salt mines' — I heard a derisive snort and was appalled to discover that it had come from *me* — 'and ordered a few beers.

'Imagine our surprise when we saw our old friend — actually, our *new* friend, Spike, sitting all by his lonesome at one of the back tables. We hadn't expected to see him here, but it seemed as if the gods were smiling on us.

'See, a couple of days ago, Spike had purchased something from me on the promise of paying for it yesterday. Unfortunately, he didn't show up when he had agreed to, so I sadly had to assume that he was going to renege on his promise.'

'And what would he have purchased from you, Mr. Snake?' Victoria was leaning forward, as if this was the most interesting tale she had ever heard in her life.

'You know, ma'am, that has entirely slipped my mind. But I do remember that he owed me some money.' He smiled.

'Ahh, it's a curse of the young, isn't it, faulty memory,' she said, returning his smile.

'Go on, Garton. And see if you can cut the crap this time.'

'Really, Deputy Wroten, such language, and with ladies present. But to continue.

'When we saw Spike sitting all alone back there, we naturally went over to say 'hello' and to *politely* remind him that he owed me money. But to our astonishment, Spike, who is usually most attentive to everything we say, wouldn't even look as us or answer us.

'We concluded that, since he had obviously been at Land's End for some time, he was . . . how shall I say it delicately . . . not in full possession of his faculties.'

'Oh, dear. I was afraid of something like that,' Victoria said, shaking her head.

'Yes. Well, we felt it incumbent upon us, as his friends, to help him out in any way we could, and since it was stuffy and warm inside, we assisted him outside where he could breathe fresh, clean, wholesome air.'

'And where you could no doubt bring up the subject of the missing payment,' Wroten added for him.

'Yes, I'm sure the subject came up at some point. We spoke with Spike for a few minutes but since he made no effort to pay what he owed and indeed seemed to become even drunker by the minute — no doubt he has a weak head for liquor — we decided to let well enough alone and we headed on home.

'Does that answer your questions,

Deputy Wroten?' Garton asked, wide-eyed, the picture of injured innocence.

'So there was no . . . uh, discussion of *consequences* for his not having the money?'

'That too may have come up at some point. I really don't remember the conversation that clearly.'

Wroten pointed to Snake's hand, which was lying open on the table. It looked as if the rattler were about to slither off his flesh and coil itself in the middle of the table.

'You seem to have injured your hand.' Not a question, merely an observation.

Snake raised his hand, closed it into a fist, and studied the crusted scrapes along his knuckles.

'Oh that. Yes, I had a flat on my car yesterday and had a bitch . . . a bit of trouble getting the nuts off the bolts. You know how difficult tight nuts can be.' He grinned at Wroten.

'Mr. Snake, was there anyone else in the parking lot during your discussion with Mr. Spike?' Victoria asked.

'No, ma'am. Just me and my friends.

But I assure you that Spike was perfectly fine when we left him. I think he was considering ways he might find the money he owes me.'

'I seriously doubt that, Mr. Snake.'

'And why would you doubt that, ma'am. All you have to do to find out the truth is ask Spike. I'm sure he will tell you that everything I've said is exactly the way it happened.'

'Well,' Victoria said, drawing the word out. Apparently Wroten had decided to let her step in at this point. I still worried about her, though. She was playing a dangerous game with a man who I was certain was as vicious and deadly as his chosen namesake. 'Because, you see, Mr. Spike can't talk to us.'

There was a momentary tightening of skin around Snake's eyes, as if the sudden thought had crossed his mind that he and the others might have gone too far the night before. Johansson might be in the hospital or something.

'Too hung over, is he?' Snake asked.

'Too dead,' Wroten said, his voice snapping out the words.

'Dead?'

'As a doornail,' Wroten said.

'Alas,' Snake said, looking abruptly down-hearted but otherwise himself again, calm and cool and in control. 'Then I shall never be able to collect my money.'

Wroten slammed his hand down on the table. The resounding *crack* echoed through the room, startling all of us. Even so, Snake was the first to recover.

He stared directly into Wroten's eyes, unblinking and unfazed.

'Alcohol poisoning, no doubt. Some-one should have warned him.'

10

'Alcohol poisoning, my ass,' Wroten roared. 'You know good and well what killed Eric Johansson.'

Snake's face remained blank, his eyes expressionless and cold.

'No, sir. That I do not.'

Wroten straightened up and glared down at Snake. The man's hand was back on the table top, serpent's head glowering at Victoria who was still staring at Snake as if she were hypnotized by him.

Maybe he really is a snake, I thought abruptly.

'Yes,' Wroten said more calmly. 'Yes, you do.'

'Then what killed him?'

Wroten leaned over until his face was level with Snake's 'You did. You and your little group of merry men. You took him outside when he was too drunk to defend himself, and you beat and pummeled and kicked him until he was nearly unconscious and then you left him there, helpless on the gravel, and went off to God-knows-where to celebrate your having taught the city punk a lesson.'

It came out rushed, almost in a single breath.

I was stunned, and I already knew what had happened to poor Eric. I could not imagine how Snake would be able to shake the accusation off as if nothing had happened.

But he did.

'No, sir. I did not.'

'Of course,' Wroten continued, as if Snake had never spoken, 'I could get into a heap of trouble if I said things like that just because I think you're an inhuman lowlife who gets his kicks by destroying the lives of innocents.'

'Yes, sir, you surely could.'

'That's why I gave you the chance to speak first, to see if you would come clean and tell the truth. Since you didn't, let me tell you a few things that might change your story a bit.'

He reached into a pocket on his jacket

and pulled out the small plastic bag with the white powder.

'Look familiar?'

He tossed it onto the center of the table.

Snake leaned over and pretended to study it closely. I noticed, however, that his hand never moved, never even came near touching it. Finger prints? I wondered.

'No. I've never seen that before in my life. What is it? Sugar?'

'Right. Like you have no idea what that is or how it came into Eric Johansson's possession.'

'No idea. And no idea.'

I was amazed at the insolence in Snake's voice. If I had been Wroten, I would probably have had the guy on the floor and been halfway through the process of beating the truth out of him . . .

But wait, that was what Snake had done to Eric, wasn't it.

I tried to calm myself and listen with as much control as Wroten was showing. Victoria still stared raptly at Snake.

I swear her head was moving slightly in time to his movements.

I shivered again.

At least I could be a bit more understanding toward Deputy Allen the next time I saw him.

'So you wouldn't recognize cocaine when you saw it?'

'That's cocaine?' Again Snake leaned forward for a closer look. 'It doesn't seem all that dangerous does it? Maybe Spike just didn't know how to handle it?'

That seemed like a tacit admission to me, but I'm not the law. Thank heavens.

'Or maybe Spike just didn't know how to handle his pusher? Maybe he didn't quite believe you when you threatened to beat him to death unless he came up with the money.'

'Now that would truly be stupid, wouldn't it, Deputy Wroten? If I were selling drugs — which I'm not, of course — and *if* Spike bought some from me — which he did not — and then *if* he didn't pay me like he agreed, why would I kill him? — which I did not. That would be the fastest way I can think of to be sure I'd never see a penny of what he — hypothetically, of course — owed me.'

'But it would be the fastest way you could think of to make sure that any other deadbeat druggies paid up fast.'

''Deadbeat druggies'? Really? Should you be talking about law-abiding citizens like that, Deputy Wroten?'

He leaned all the way back in his chair, clasping his hands behind his head to show his utter disregard for everything Wroten was saying to him.

I wanted to kick the legs out from under the chair and watch him slam down on his head.

All right, I wasn't as calm as I should have been.

But then, I had seen what Snake and his gang had done to Eric.

I wasn't sure I'd be able to get to sleep easily for a long while.

Snake put one booted foot up onto the table and crossed the other over it. It was as if he were baiting Wroten.

If so, Wroten snapped up the bait.

'What do you think I would find if I took those fancy boots of yours to the crime lab down-mountain and had the techs spend a couple of days with them?'

'Well,' Snake said coolly, 'I expect they would find dirt and maybe a touch of cow shit on them, since I mostly walk around in your town.'

'And here?' Wroten pointed to the polished edges where the steel toes were snugged against the leather.'

'Not much more. Maybe some polish. Even a little bit of high-test metal cleaner. They looked a bit dullish yesterday, so I spent a long time polishing them to bring out that just-like-new sparkle.'

'No traces of human blood? Of Eric's blood?'

Snake jerked upright in his chair, his feet falling to the ground with a thump.

'And if they did? What of it.' Now there was a solid emotion in his voice cutting through the coldness. 'Spike was throwing up like a baby by the time we got him outside in the fresh air, really puking up his guts, you know. Who knows, maybe I stepped in some of the vomit, maybe there was blood in it. People do that, you know, get so shit-faced that when they throw up they break little blood vessels in their throat and then there's blood in the vomit.

'Who's to say that's not what happened with Spike?'

'Who's to say I shouldn't arrest you on suspicion of murder?'

'Murder?' Snake sounded honestly offended. 'You have one witness back there who will swear that Spike made it back into the bar long after me and my friends took off. You have another one who will swear that he drove Spike home, drunk out of his gourd and maybe a bit banged up from falling on his face in the parking lot. But you don't have a single witness to say that I ever laid so much as a hand on him.'

'You seem to know a lot about what happened *after* you left. I think maybe you've been so worried about going overboard that you and your cronies rushed back here first thing in the morning to make sure that when you beat Eric Johansson nearly senseless you didn't also . . . '

'Kill him? You can't make a case for

murder. That's pretty clear to me. I think it would be just as clear to a lawyer.'

Snake grinned.

'And you can't make a case for me dealing drugs, either. No witnesses, remember. The only one you know of who could testify that it was me — hypothetically, again — is dead. And I sure as hell didn't kill him.' Another sudden spurt of anger surged through Snake's voice. 'You can't even charge me with beating the kid.'

He leaned forward and glared directly at Wroten as he almost spat out the words: 'No witnesses.'

He settled back into the chair.

'You can't arrest me for anything, Dep-u-ty Wroten. Not a thing.'

'Deputy,' I said suddenly, unable to hold it back, 'can't you just arrest him for being an unspeakable little bas . . . '

'Lynn, dear,' Victoria said, the first words she had spoken for some minutes now. It wasn't like her to be silent for so long. 'You shouldn't say things like that. Deputy Wroten knows the law better than you or I.' She was still staring into

Snake's eyes when she spoke. It made her look as if she were an automaton, capable of saying only what he wanted her to say.

'There are such things as rules of evidence, acceptable police procedures, and, as Mr. Snake rightly points out, witnesses. Deputy Wroten is bound by the law to behave in a certain way.

'Isn't he, Mr. Snake?'

Snake glanced at her as if surprised to find that she was on his side.

'Right as rain, ma'am. Right as rain.'

'And as much as we might find it distasteful,' here Victoria pushed her chair back and stood, her eyes never breaking contact with Snake's, 'we must abide by the law. Even if we know that Mr. Snake here beat a young man nearly to death over a matter of a few dollars and a few grains of cocaine.'

Snake didn't look quite as comfortable as he had a moment before.

Victoria continued walking around the table, until she was standing right next to Snake, even a bit too close, invading his personal space for reasons I could not begin to figure out. She leaned over

— although she was enough shorter than he that she didn't have to lean far, even when he was sitting — and continued speaking directly into his face.

'Even when we know that you are dealing drugs from this hell-hole, Eddie. Even when we know that your dear mother and father would be so embarrassed if they knew what was going on right now that they would hide their faces in shame, Eddie.'

There was a bright red glow in Snake's cheeks now, a flush that was accompanied by a sharp increase in his rate of breath. I could hear the air pushing in and out of his lungs.

Victoria leaned even closer. Her nose almost touched his — almost, but not quite. Her voice remained as quiet and calm and controlled as ever.

'Even though poor Eric Johansson, beaten and bruised and bloody in his bed, cold and stiff and dead is still worth more than twice what you are, Little Eddie, living and breathing and warm and . . . '

'Get out of my face, you old witch!' Snake — only now he was more Edward

Garton than he was Snake — yelled at her. 'Shut up! You ... ' Instead of finishing his sentence, he raised his right arm — serpent twisting and coiling and twining as if it were alive — and thrust it, palm forward, directly into Victoria's chest.

With a sharp little cry, she went over backward, landing on her back on the filthy floor.

For an instant, everyone froze, including Victoria. Her eyes were wide, startled looking, and her lips formed a tight, 'Oh.'

Then the stasis broke.

Carver leaped off the stool and came across the room at a run.

'Miz Sears! Miz Sears!' he cried as he knelt beside her and put his arm around her shoulders and tried to support her while she seemed to gasp for breath.

The cluster of men at the doorway surged a few steps forward at their fearless leader's heroic action — strong-arming a helpless old woman — but snapped to a halt when Deputy Wroten looked their way and pulled his service weapon from his holster. He didn't point it at them, but the message was clear. *Back off. Now!*

Garton had pulled himself as far back in his chair as possible and was pointing at Victoria with his left hand — untattooed but still the hand of a strong, muscular, and vigorous young man — and was bleating, 'You saw that, Wroten, you saw that, she provoked me, she shoved her face right into mine and she . . . '

'Oh shut up, you pathetic loser,' I said. 'No one wants to listen to your excuses for being a bullying liar.'

I hurried around and, kneeling at Victoria's other side, helped Carver as she tried to stand up. It took several attempts but at last she was standing on her own. She took a tentative step, winced, and put her hand on her hip as if to say, 'Well, that truly and honestly hurts. But it could be worse. He could have broken it.'

As soon as she was upright and stable, she took a step toward Garton. He rose to his full height and glared down at her, but it didn't make a bit of difference. There was no question now as to who was in charge.

'Edward, that was a foolish thing to do. But you were always doing foolish things, even as a boy. Now you are doing foolish things as a man.

'Selling drugs to children.

'Threatening people who don't do as you wish.

'Beating up smaller men, bringing in your gang to join with you.'

'Assaulting little old ladies who never raised a hand against you.'

'Hey, wait a minute,' Garton yelped. 'Assault! I never . . . I didn't . . . '

'Officer Wroten,' Victoria said, just as primly as she had spoken to Rafferty the first time she entered the bar, with just as much sweet-little-old-lady-who-wouldn't-hurt-a-fly intonation in her voice as she had demonstrated when Edward Garton first spoke to us, 'do I need to swear out a formal assault charge now, or can it wait until we get back to Fox Creek?'

'Well, ma'am,' Wroten responded, a touch of John Wayne in his voice and his cuffs hanging from one hand, 'Since you have a room full of *witnesses* that this man shoved you to the floor when you had made no physical threat against him, and especially since one of those *witnesses* is a sworn officer of the law, I guess we can cuff him here and take care of the paperwork later.'

11

'That's all well and good,' Victoria said from her padded seat in one of the booths at the back of Land's End. It was more comfortable for her, since her hip really had taken quite a smack against the hardwood floor.

'He will be where you want him when you get the coroner's report back on poor Eric . . . '

'Safely in jail,' I added.

'Yes, Lynn dear, where he should be. But Richard dear, don't you see that it would be no good trying to accuse him of murdering Eric Johansson.'

'Not murder, no. We couldn't prove intent. But manslaughter . . . '

'Not even that. I'm afraid, Richard, that all that poor benighted young man is guilty of is aggravated assault and battery. *All!* Listen to me. He and his cronies — who should also be charged . . . '

'They will be. They're in the other

room with strict orders to behave themselves. Carver's keeping an eye on them. I've let them know in the strongest possible terms that if they cause any trouble, the charges will go up according-ly. They're already falling all over each other pointing fingers of guilt.'

He cast a glance at Garton, who was sitting by himself at one of the tables along the wall. He was the only one in the place besides the three of us, and Rafferty over behind the bar. The two old fellows who had been here during Wroten's interrogation of Garton had disappeared right after the action had settled down.

Garton was securely cuffed to a metal pipe extending from floor to ceiling. He didn't look particularly comfortable with one arm hanging at about shoulder height, but I don't think it was painful.

Too bad.

Victoria followed Wroten's gaze.

'It's so sad. He and his cronies beat a defenseless and exceedingly vulnerable young man, they kicked him with steel-capped boots, they caused him gross bodily harm, and they left him alone and injured on the parking lot.'

'Right. So?'

'Well, I'm afraid, Richard dear, that they didn't actually *kill* Eric.'

Wroten sighed and slumped back in his chair.

'I like it better, I think, when you refer to me more formally as Deputy Wroten or even as just plain Wroten. That means you're with me. But the moment you start in with 'Richard dear', that means I've blown it somehow. And you're going to tell me how.

'Not exactly *blown it*, Richa . . . Deputy Wroten.' She smiled. Her smile could be disarming even when you knew that she was about to let go with both barrels. 'Just . . . uh . . . *misinterpreted* several crucial facts.

'You see, I think I know why Eric Johansson died, what actually killed him, and where I can find the instrument of his death. But you are going to have to trust me for a bit longer.'

'Do I have a choice?'

'Not really, because you have to see the entire string of events completely or it won't make sense.'

'When will the van be here to pick up Groton and his merry men?' I wanted to know in part because I wanted to get on with whatever Victoria had in mind and in part because if it was going to take more than half an hour or so, I was going to borrow Wroten's gun, march over to the bar, and insist that Rafferty do something about finding me some food. I was starving.

Wroten checked his wristwatch.

'Maybe an hour. Maybe less. As soon as possible but with Allen still out at the Johanssons' we're a little short-handed. They may have to call in a couple of off-duties to help out.'

'Fine,' Victoria said. 'In the meantime, Lynn dear, why don't you go over and check with Mr. Rafferty and see if he has any sandwiches or anything for lunch.'

'Sure.' Sometimes I think Victoria is a mind-reader. It didn't bother me this time, though.

I got up and crossed to the bar.

No, Rafferty told me, he didn't usually stock anything for lunches since Land's

End didn't officially open until later in the afternoon, but yes, he could 'rustle up something' like he did for some of the old guys who wandered in during the day. He'd check.

He disappeared through a door that presumably led from behind the bar into a store-room.

I waited at the bar for a couple of minutes, munching on a handful of peanuts from a none-too-clean glass bowl.

'This is all I could find,' Rafferty said when he returned bearing a small tray. On it were four or five sandwiches and three bottles of orange soda. 'They're ham and cheese. And I found the pop in the back of the fridge. Don't know how long it's been there but I figured you'd prefer it to beer, Deputy Wroten being on duty and all.'

'What do we owe you?' I started to check in my handbag for my change purse.

'On the house, ma'am. You being part of the official investigation and all.'

Yes, and the fact that Wroten had said

nothing more to him about his responsibilities — legal, ethical, or moral — for what had happened to Eric Johansson no doubt made him feel so relieved that he would have served up a seven-course dinner if he'd had the materials and the equipment.

I thanked him and returned to the booth with the food.

Victoria and Wroten were in the middle of an exchange but I had no difficulty figuring out what they were talking about.

'So, Eric Johansson *was* killed.' It sounded as if he was satisfied that at least that datum had been established as fact.

'Yes.' Victoria said firmly.

'But he didn't die from the beating?'

'No. I'm sure that what Garton and the others did certainly was contributory, but I'm equally sure that when he examines the body the coroner will find that it wasn't the actual cause of death.'

'But he was *killed*.'

'Oh yes, this was not — what's the phrase — a 'death by natural causes.'' Victoria was adamant on that point.

'He just wasn't killed by Garton and the others?'

'No. Not directly.'

'There you go again, Miz Sears.' Wroten half-laughed. 'If I didn't know you better, I would say that you were trying to weasel out of what you just said a minute ago.'

Victoria smiled back. 'No weaseling, Richard. Just being careful and precise.'

'And Ellis had nothing to do with it at all.'

'Heavens, no. The boy was just trying to be a good neighbor. I doubt if he had any idea that young Johansson was connected with drugs or with anything else Garton and his gang might have pressured that poor boy into.'

'But others were involved? It wasn't anything like a suicide?'

'Yes, several others had to have been involved.'

Wroten slapped his hand on the table, more a gesture of half-hearted frustration than the outright explosion of anger he'd shown before.

'You know, Miz Sears, if it were anyone

157

but you trying to play Twenty Questions with me in the middle of a murder investigation, I'd probably hit them with an obstruction charge and get my spare cuffs from the car and slap them on.'

'I'm sure you would. But you wouldn't do such a thing to a sweet little old thing like me, now would you?' She cocked her head and batted her eyes so outrageously that both Wroten and I burst out laughing.

'No,' Wroten said. 'I guess I wouldn't. But you still won't identify them, won't let me go talk to them, question them, arrest them if there's enough evidence?'

'None of that would do you any good. They won't be able to tell you anything. And there certainly won't be any evidence of *murder*.'

'But they — these mysterious great unknowns — *were* involved?'

'Absolutely.'

'How sure are you of all of this, Miz Sears?' The laughter of a moment before had dissipated. Things were serious again. A young man was dead, and the woman in front of him claimed to know how.

'Very sure, Deputy Wroten.'

Wroten leaned back.

'Well, I guess we'll just have to wait for the van and get this crew taken care of, won't we.'

'That seems appropriate. There is really no rush. I don't think any of the others will try to 'make a break for it' as they say on television. And I'm quite sure the evidence you will need will still be there.

'Lynn dear, we must be sure to thank Mr. Rafferty for these sandwiches. They are really quite lovely.' She reached for another.

It didn't take a full hour. Probably forty minutes later, the van pulled up. Victoria and I remained where we were in the booth as Wroten unlocked the cuffs from the pipe and refitted them to Garton's other arm — the one with the rattlesnake — and escorted him out the door.

There must have been a patrol car waiting because a few minutes later we heard a car leave the parking lot and Wroten and another deputy entered Land's End. They went directly into the back room and emerged with four sullen-looking young men. The suspects must have talked themselves out. They certainly weren't talking now.

Carver followed, just behind the two deputies. He accompanied them outside, and another few minutes passed before Wroten and Carver re-entered the bar and walked over to where we were waiting.

'Well, ladies, are you ready?'

'I believe so, Deputy Wroten. Do you need anything before we leave, Lynn dear?'

I shook my head. At this point I was too interested in what was about to happen to want any more delays. Victoria had steadfastly refused to answer any of my questions about Johansson's death while we waited. Instead, she kept turning our conversation back to more mundane issues — the state of the weather, the ongoing harvest, the latest news from among her friends in Fox Creek.

Yes, I was ready.

12

Victoria spoke to Deputy Wroten for a few minutes, out of earshot of either Carver or myself. We waited for them in the cool shade of the plane trees — we called them 'sycamores' down-mountain, back where I had left my old life, but up here in Fox Creek everyone used the simpler name.

I leaned against the massive trunk, allowing my fingers to wander up and down the mottled bark. The bits felt like puzzle pieces, each slightly different from the next but all about the same general size and shape. Some were green, some brown or grey.

Kind of like my life.

I'd not had much time to myself today, what with Victoria's unexpected call, and then finding the boy's body and being shuttled from house to house, then driving to Neilson's farm, then out here to Land's End, so these few moments were the first time I was alone with my thoughts.

Carver was staring off toward the mountains, so I decided that perhaps he was doing some soul-searching as well.

I had thought of Terry and Shawn today, once in direct conjunction with a sudden and terrible death, and it hadn't devastated me. They had left my life nearly fifteen months before, and for most of that time I had believed that my own life was essentially, fundamentally over. I felt like a remnant from some horrible fairy-tale-turned-tragedy, another body to litter the blood-choked stage once it realized that it had nothing left to live for.

Then I had met Victoria Sears, and as luck, Fortune, or God would have it, on the same day another body had been found. She knew about my personal grief but had not spoken of it, had instead treated me as someone whole and uninjured and healthy . . . and by the end of that day, I realized that I had become at least in part what she thought of me. I had faced death in the present and in the past, and had lived through both.

Now the same thing had happened again — or near enough the same thing — and what had I done?

I had remembered, not Terry's battered body or Shawn's untouched toys still haunting the shelves and drawers of his bedroom in my house down-mountain, but both of them — my man and my little man — laughing and alive and full of love.

And the memory had not hurt.

It had felt good.

I almost wanted to rush back to Estelle and Edgar's place and dig my jewelry box out of the big drawer at the bottom of the old-fashioned dresser, remove the small twist of paper that contained the three unset blue calcite stones, and keep one of them in my pocket to touch whenever or wherever I wanted.

Or more, to put on the necklace and earrings, not even changing out of my jeans and work-a-day blouse, and wear them proudly and lovingly and . . . most crucially . . . *happily*.

All of this, on the day that Eric Johansson died and I was following

Victoria around again, on the trail of a killer.

I still missed my men.

I still loved them.

But I could — I *would* — go on with my life without them by my side.

Because they were both still alive in my heart and in my memory.

'Miz Hanson?' Wroten's deep voice broke into my reverie.

He was standing at the door of his patrol car, one foot balanced on the frame. The man of action. Ready to head out and catch the bad guys.

'Coming,' I called. Carver turned toward the patrol car at the same time and we crossed the parking lot together.

I don't know what he had been thinking about — or perhaps I do — but we smiled, almost shyly, at each other as we walked.

No words were needed.

We each had our memories.

'I'd like you two to ride with Miz Sears in your car, if you don't mind, Miz Hanson.'

'It's Lynn, and of course I'll drive. I'll

follow you, okay.'

He nodded and got in. No silliness about Carver having to be in the same car with him. Carver had nothing to do with the death of his friend.

Wroten pulled out onto the State Highway and I followed.

'We're going to Mr. Neilson's place,' Victoria said, 'but not the same way we came. We're going to take the back roads. It's a little longer but I think it will be instructive for us ... and for Deputy Wroten. If he keeps his eyes open.'

'For what?' Carver asked from the seat behind me.

'For evidence. For this and that ... ' And she said no more.

We followed the State Highway for a mile or so, then I saw Wroten's blinker winking away to let us know that he was turning onto a narrow dirt road that led arrow-straight between the barbed wire fences that formed the boundaries of two fields.

This close to the highway, the slight gullies on both sides of the road had been mowed close, short enough that I could see that the ground was dark and moist. Lingering runoff from the last rains, perhaps, or seepage from the irrigation ditches that surrounded the two fields.

The further from the highway we went, the thicker and taller the growth in the ditches became, until at last the milk-weeds and sunflowers and occasional stands of wild roses — complete with small, five-petaled pink blossoms — nearly blocked the fields from our vision.

After a mile or so, we turned onto another dirt road, this one slightly wider and more hard-packed, but otherwise just the same as the first. Then, after another mile, another turn.

Apparently the fields in this part of the valley were laid out in a grid of squares, each a half- or a quarter-mile on a side, with access roads running between many of the properties. Made sense. Easier that way to get tractors and other needed equipment to all of the fields.

'There's another one,' Victoria said abruptly, gesturing with her hand.

'Another what?' My attention was pretty much focused on the road and out of the corner of my eye I could see nothing untoward.

'That one was a frog, I believe.' She said. The comment did little to resolve my confusion.

'You're counting frogs?'

'Yes. And not just frogs. So far I've seen several field mice, a garter snake, and a something that might have been a weasel.'

'Running across the road, you mean? I haven't seen anything.'

'No, ma'am,' Carver said from the back seat. 'I think Miz Sears is counting road kill. Bodies. Crushed by the tractors and pickups that come this way.'

I couldn't help but stare for a moment at Victoria.

'But why in the world . . . ?'

'Yeah, why would you . . . ?' Carver began his question at the same time I did.

'We used to tally road kill when I was a little girl walking to school. At least the boys did. Ah, another field mouse.' She pointed, and this time I glanced quickly enough to note something dusty brown and flat and matted just as it passed beneath the front hood. If I hadn't been looking I would not have seen it. It matched the color and texture of the dirt road almost perfectly.

'Yeah,' Carver said. He laughed. 'We did that, too, when I was a kid. Back when I was in, oh I don't know, fourth or fifth grade, something like that, we had a really wet spring. All the ditches were full of water and the ground was marshy almost everywhere.

'I had to walk about two miles to school . . . '

'By the time you're my age, that will have become at least five miles, and uphill both ways,' Victoria said, smiling.

'Yeah, well, it seemed like a long ways back then. Anyway, there were frogs everywhere, and this one day we started to count them. They were mostly flat and dried up, kind of like moldy jerky, but now and then we'd spot a squishy one.'

'Ugh.' I couldn't help it. The picture he was drawing was not particularly pleasant.

'Yeah. We counted them, though, and by the time we got to school, we had seen over a hundred. Flat-frogs, we called them.'

I thought that was the end of the story because he fell silent for a while.

'On the way home, one of the guys, Skip Waite, he decided that the flat-frogs looked kind of like weird-shaped Frisbees, so he scooped one up and gave it a fling. It didn't fly quite as well as a store-bought Frisbee but it actually did pretty well.

'One of the girls, Katy Whittaker, was a year or two younger than the rest of us and she squealed like she had just been stuck with a pin. So, of course, that set Skip off, and for the rest of the walk home, he was whizzing flat-frogs at all of the girls that passed.'

'I suspect that didn't set well with quite a few parents,' I said.

'Well, as I recall, Skip didn't look too comfortable when he sat down the next day at school and he didn't toss any more flat-frogs, so I guess you're right.'

'I know Katy Whittaker,' Victoria said. 'Sweet thing. Grew up into a real beauty. And I think that she just got engaged to a fine, handsome young man of my acquaintance. Name of Mr. Skip Waite.

So I expect there was no lasting harm done. And both of them will probably have some interesting stories to tell their children when they ask 'Dad, how did you meet Mom?''

By then I had noticed a few other odd-shaped bits of flotsam on the road that might have been partially flattened dirt clods . . . or other things.

'Okay, Victoria, why are you counting those things?'

'I think that one might have been a shrew. It's so hard to tell once they've been . . . flattened.'

'Victoria!'

'Well, the number of poor creatures lying dead on the road is, in a way, important to the farmers. Right now, we are having one of the best summers for some time. Spring was wet, so there's plenty of water for the crops, like that year Carver was talking about.

'Plenty of water means that the crops will do well. And that, in turn, means that there will probably be an excess of vermin to scavenge for food as harvest time draws near. Field mice, of course, and frogs and lizards in the damper parts, like the run-off ditches along these back roads. Badgers and even some birds will raid the fields when they think it's safe.'

I was pleased for the horticulture lesson, I suppose, but I really wanted to know what Victoria was up to. Certainly she had a reason for this rather strange conversation. After all, how many near-octogenarians pass the time in the car by counting 'flat-frogs'.

'Victoria . . . ' I tried again.

But to no avail.

'Of course, cows don't generally break through the fences to eat wheat once it is ripening. Farmers try to keep that from happening anyway. They can eat the young plants — the cows, I mean, of course, not the farmers — but once the wheat ripens it becomes a danger to them. If they gorge on too much, it can cause bloating, and if the bloating is serious enough, the cattle will die.

'I remember once one of my uncles had a cow that had bloated on wheat and he had to take a pocket knife and cut . . . '

'Victoria, please. Flat-frogs are enough. I don't need a picture of a bleeding bloated cow in my mind right now.

'And besides, I think we can be fairly certain that our victim did not die of over-indulgence in ripe wheat, can't we.'

'Ah . . . yes, to be sure. Sorry, Lynn dear. I'm afraid I got a bit carried away with my story. Anyway, if there are a great many vermin in the fields, that also means that those creatures that depend on them for their own sustenance will also flourish: shrews, foxes, a variety of snakes, hawks, owls. Even other, larger species of mice and rats. At night you can hear . . .

'Oh, wait. Deputy Wroten is pulling in at the Neilson place. Right here, Lynn dear. Be careful, though, this old bridge is rather narrow for your car.'

I managed to maneuver the car over the six-foot long plank bridge that led from the last of our back-country roads — this one at least graveled — to a break in the fence. Not far from where we entered the field, I saw the cluster of machinery that had been there that morning, as well as a handful of men, apparently waiting for Deputy Wroten to return.

Okay, here we were.

Now what?

13

Wroten was the first to get out of his vehicle. We waited in my car until he had approached the men, shaken hands around, and spoken to them for a few moments. Then he gave us a come-on-over gesture and we piled out of our car.

It was hard walking, making our way through the inches-high stubble and across the remains of old irrigation tracks. Once or twice I nearly stumbled and more than once felt my ankle twist on a loose clod.

I silently thanked heaven for hiking boots.

And once — I'm sure of it — I saw a mouse streak past my foot and disappear into the maze of stubble and tumbled straw that halfway hid the ground.

But we all made it over to where Wroten was standing, whole and in one piece.

'Now what's all this, Wroten,' Tom

Neilson asked, not aggressively but not quite as politely as he might have had the officer just happened to stop by to shoot the breeze.

'Well, I'm going to let Miz Sears here do most of the talking because it was all her idea and she knows best what she's looking for. But she says that the answer to how the Johansson boy died is right here in your field. And that we can find it if we look for it right now. Once the harvest gets under way again, it might be lost, or at least it will be a mite more difficult to find. Okay?'

Neilson nodded, more perplexed than anything.

'Okay, Miz Sears. It's all yours,' he said, gesturing to the field. 'What do you need?'

'Thank you, Tom. The first thing we will have to do is extract that flatbed of yours from the ditch.'

'But you said this morning to leave everything as it was,' Wroten broke in.

'Yes, I did. And thank you, Tom, for doing that. But now it's time to resolve a mystery, and we can do that best with the flatbed on level ground.'

'I don't know, ma'am,' Neilson said, removing his hat and scratching the back of his neck — a stereotype and a cliché, I know, but that is where stereotypes and clichés come from . . . from the things people do when they aren't thinking about what they are doing.

'I don't know. We pull that truck out wrong and the axle might completely collapse. That might mean spending . . . '

'Oh, don't worry about that,' Victoria said lightly. 'This is part of an official investigation into the death of a citizen of Fox Creek. I'm sure Deputy Wroten can figure out a way to help you cover any additional expenses.'

Wroten looked as startled as if someone had surreptitiously hooked him up to a couple of electrodes and suddenly hit the 'on' switch. His head jerked toward Victoria so hard that I thought I heard something snap.

'Now look here, Victoria, you can't just go around . . . ' He paused, sighed, and turned back to face Neilson. 'Just do as she says. In the long run, that's the easiest way.'

'Whatever you want, ma'am. But even so it's going to be tricky. All I've got here is that old pickup, my combine, and my baler. And I'm not sure any of them has enough *oomph* to do much good.'

'Hmmm, yes. But perhaps if Deputy Wroten would use his patrol car, along with the pickup . . .'

Wroten was shaking his head but he was already on his way to his patrol car, where he extracted a long chain and a length of thick rope from the trunk.

Neilson had pulled a similar hank of rope from behind the driver's seat of the pickup.

It took them three tries, what with the angle of the flatbed truck, the depth of the irrigation ditch, and the damp, at times slimy ground in the field as water from the ditch splashed over the banks and spread along the nearly flat soil.

Wheels spun in the mud, making more mud. Twice the flatbed twisted around and seemed more likely to pull the patrol car and the pickup into the ditch with it than they were to pull it out. And once the rear ends of both the patrol car and the pickup began shimmying on the slippery soil, then sliding, and finally came within a foot or so of slamming into each other.

Victoria and I had retreated into the uncut portion of the field, where the footing was a bit firmer. Standing in the thigh-high wheat made me feel a good bit uncomfortable, since I could not see what might be scampering across my feet to the accompaniment of the roar of the engines, the occasional shriek of metal against metal — I didn't know and didn't *want* to know what was causing that — the flapping of tires throwing up great gobbets of mud from the runoff of the irrigation ditch, and the, unfortunately, more than frequent and often extraordinarily colorful sounds of frustrated men pulling and straining.

At last, however, the flatbed was freed. Even out of the ditch it canted noticeably toward the front, but apparently that did not bother Victoria.

'Fine,' she said. 'Good job. Well done.'

I half expected to see her brush her palms together as if to get rid of any dust, but instead she simply walked over to where Wroten, Neilson, and the rest of the men were standing.

I followed.

Everyone except Victoria and I was spattered with mud and red-faced from exertion. Even Carver had a long streak of dirt on his cheek, and Deputy Wroten's service trousers were damp around the cuffs. From where I had been standing, it had seemed that moving the flatbed had been a difficult and arduous job.

Apparently it had been worse than that.

Victoria stood back a few paces and examined the flatbed, nodding a couple of times. Then she turned to Neilson.

'May I borrow several of your men? Three or four should do.'

'Whatever you need.'

'Thank you.'

She examined the men carefully, running her eyes up and down the legs of their jeans. I didn't know what she was looking for but apparently it was something quite specific, because all at once she touched one man lightly on the shoulder.

'Do you have your work gloves?'

'Yes, ma'am.'

'May I see them?'

He pulled a pair of leather gloves from his back pocket and extended them, rather tentatively, it seemed, to Victoria. She took them and studied them closely, even running one of her fingers up and down a couple of the seams.

'They look fine. Would you mind standing over by the flatbed, please?'

The man looked at Wroten, who shrugged minimally, then at Neilson who gave a nod of acquiescence, then at the other men, who just looked puzzled and confused. Finally he walked over and leaned against the passenger door of the cab.

Victoria followed the procedure with three others. Carver had offered to help do whatever it was she wanted done, but when she asked about work gloves, he shook his head.

'Left them at home,' he said.

'I'm sorry, dear. I know you want to help, you want to find out what happened to Eric, but you really can't do it barehanded.'

Carver knew her even better than I did. He didn't even try to argue. He simply stepped back out of the way and let her continue choosing men.

When there were four men lined up by the flatbed, she asked Mr. Neilson to back the pick-up close to the tailgate of the flatbed.

That done, she picked two of the men, seemingly at random, to mount the flatbed.

'Now,' she said when they were in position. 'Please listen to me carefully. *Very* carefully. I want you to lift the bales on the truck, one at a time, one of you lifting from each end *using the baling twine only*. Is that clear?'

Thoroughly nonplussed the two men agreed, yes that was clear, although *why* they were doing it remained a mystery.

'I want you to hand each bale off to two men in the back of the pick-up.' She gestured, and the remaining men clambered into the empty pick-up bed. 'Again, very carefully. By the baling twine.'

The four men stood for a moment as if anticipating further instructions. At a nod from Victoria, however, they began the task.

The first two men strode to the first bale.

When the truck had slid into the irrigation ditch the afternoon before, it had been about one-third loaded. None of the bales had slid out of position when it went in, which meant that there were three rows of bales across the front end of the bed, three bales per row, four bales high.

Thirty-six bales.

With exquisite care, as if they were handling a case of ten-year-old sweating dynamite, the two men slid their gloved fingers beneath the baling twine on each end of the top bale in the first row. Together they lifted just enough that the bale cleared the one beneath, then they swung it sideways and let it drop to the worn planks on the bed.

At another nod from Victoria, they lifted it again and, backs bent so that the bale was only inches from the wooden planks, carried it to the end of the bed and passed it over to the two in the pickup.

They slid their fingers under the lifted twine, barely even touching the straw beneath, and then lowered it, short end facing the pickup cab, until it rested on the pickup's metal bed.

'Perfect,' Victoria said.

I could tell that, even though the men might not be taking her totally seriously, she was tense about . . . well, about *something*.

'Now, still being *very careful*, I want you to rotate the bale on the long axis so that I can examine all four of the long sides. But please, *only* using the twine.'

By this time, Wroten had helped her onto the pickup's extended tailgate where she had an unobstructed view of the bale. The rest of us were gathered along the sides so we could see also.

And see we did.

Four sides of a bale of hay.

Just long, narrow threads of straw that had been captured by the baler and tied together into a compact block.

When the fourth side lay upward and Victoria had had a chance to study it, she straightened, placed one hand against her spine as if stooping had caused her some bit of pain, and said, 'Not this one.'

'Do you want us to stack the bales here on the pickup?,' one of the men asked.

'No, I think not. Mr. Neilson, is it all right if I ask the rest of you to remove each bale as I examine it and place them . . . oh, wherever you think best.'

'Will do.' He and another of his men jerked the bale out of the pickup and carried it to a fairly clear dry spot a dozen or so yards from where we were working.

While they were doing that, Victoria turned back to the two men still on the flatbed, and said, rather chirpily, I thought, 'One down, thirty-five to go.'

Of course, we didn't have to go through all thirty-five.

Fifteen were enough.

Victoria never let down her diligence.

When one of the men on the flatbed lost his grip on the twine and made to reach under the bale to secure his hold, she hollered, 'No. Let it fall back down.'

He and the other men dropped the bale — which had happened to be on the bottom layer right on top of the flatbed

— like it was flaming hot.

Both jerked straight up and looked into each other's eyes.

I rather suspect they saw an unfamiliar flicker of panic before they settled down and each took a deep, calming breath.

'All right, now. Try again. Very carefully.'

This time neither let the bale slip.

One by one, fourteen bales were transported from the flatbed over to the pickup and turned — carefully — so that Victoria could examine every side. She never touched any of the bales. But I could tell that her sharp eyes had not missed an inch.

I didn't know what she was looking for, but it wasn't there.

The fifteenth bale was different.

The two men from the flatbed carried it over to the pickup and handed it off. Business as usual. Perhaps they were even a bit lax about taking precautions, although Victoria's repeated warnings kept them from becoming downright casual.

Fortunately for them.

The two on the pickup gave Victoria a chance to look over the top of the bale.

Then at her nod, they turned it so that the first side was up.

I think Victoria was becoming slightly unnerved as if she had expected to see . . . whatever there was to see . . . long before this. At any rate, I saw a flicker of disappointment in her eyes as the side was turned upward.

When the next side appeared — what had been the bottom of the bale as it was originally stacked — I think every one of us instinctively jumped back a step or two.

One of the men on the flatbed angled slightly to the side when he jerked back and almost went over the edge before grabbing hold of the other man's work shirt and pulling himself upright.

I gasped.

That sounds theatrical, even melodramatic, but it was the truth.

I gasped as if someone had punched me in the chest.

Emerging from the bale, right where someone trying to get a good grip to lift it up — or where someone boosting the bale with a knee to get it high enough to stack on two others, as this one had been — looking as if it were erupting from the bale's black core, jaws open and fangs protruding, was the severed head of a rattlesnake.

As they watched, horrified, the jaws twitched.

14

'Good Lord,' one of the men whispered.

'That's the one,' Victoria said softly. Then, to Deputy Wroten: 'There's your killer, officer.'

That's all it took for the men — and myself, since I am telling only truth today — to cluster back around the bed of the pickup.

The two men who had been manhandling the bale had backed to the cab window and were leaning against the pickup's roof, inspecting their gloves as if they were afraid they had somehow been infected by mere proximity to the hideous head.

Victoria remained where she had been, standing firmly on the tailgate, looking down at the instrument of Eric Johansson's death.

'Here, ma'am,' Tom Neilson said gently, 'Let me help you off of there.'

'Thank you,' Victoria said. She was shaking now. As rock-solid as she had proven all day, now that the moment of revelation had come, she suddenly seemed her age. Or almost her age.

I'm not sure *anything* will ever make Victoria Sears seem like an old woman to me.

Neilson held her arm while the two of them walked over to where I was standing. He handed her off to me, then continued around until he was standing on my other side along the bed of the pickup.

'If that don't beat all,' someone said. And from another: 'Well, I never . . . '

'I have,' Victoria said. All eyes turned to watch her. 'I grew up on a farm not far from here. My granddad and my father ran a few head of cattle, grandmother and mother had a few chickens and a fairly large truck garden that supplied a goodly number of the neighbors with vegetables and berries — especially strawberries and raspberries — during the summer months.

'I was an only child, so I became a sort of tomboy, always following either my granddad or my father around. Mom and grandma took care of the house and garden.

'I remember one day — hot, like today, toward the end of summer and the beginning of haying season — I was alone with granddad, walking the edge of the field not too far from a little creek' — she pronounced it *crick*, as I knew she would. 'Granddad was irrigating that day, so we had his old shovel with us. I was balancing it on my shoulder, trying to look grown-up.

'All of a sudden, he whipped the shovel off my shoulder and without any hesitation at all, flung it right out into the middle of the field. I followed him out to retrieve it. With that single throw, he had nearly decapitated a field mouse.

''Got to get them before they eat up all the grain,' he said, knowing I had a soft spot for 'little critters,' as he called them. I swallowed, accepting the truth of what he was saying but at the same time grieving that this little fellow's death had been seen as necessary.

''Can we bury him?' I asked.

''Sure we can, darlin', sure we can.'

'So we gathered the body up on the scoop of the shovel and carried it out a little way beyond the edge of the field, right by the creek. Granddad scooped out a little hole and nudged the body in, then covered it with a bit of earth and tamped it down with his boot.'

I noticed that several of the older men were nodding, as if the experience were familiar to them, either as children of farmers or as fathers of farm children.

Some lessons had to be learned, but they didn't have to be learned brutally.

After a short pause, Victoria continued: 'We stood for a minute near the little mound of dirt, listening to the water gurgling over the rocks in the creek, then granddad said it was getting on time to be heading home.

'I wasn't ready to leave yet. 'Can I put some flowers on the grave?' I asked.

' 'You sure you want to do that? It'll make everything seem sadder if you do.'

'But I was sure, so he gave me the okay.

'There was a big rock a short way down the creek, white granite, I remember, no doubt warm from the long day's sunshine. At the base of the rock there was a small patch of red tube-like flowers — I've since learned that they were penstemons — that I thought would be perfect.

'I was picking my miniature funeral display when my granddad suddenly called, 'Freeze, Vicky. Don't move an inch.'

'It was a tribute to how much I loved and trusted him that I did exactly as he said. Still bent over, I froze, one hand stretched half way to the tallest penstemon stem, the one I wanted as the centerpiece of my tiny bouquet.

The next thing I heard was the 'whoosh' of the shovel as it passed by me, blade first. Then I gasped as my grandfather grabbed me under the arms and with a single smooth motion swung me up to the top of the rock.

''Stay there until I tell you otherwise. Do not move!' he whispered as he hesitated for an instant to make sure I wouldn't fall, then ran off into the low brush at the edge of the field.

'The rock was three feet high or so, with a broad, almost flat top — probably one of the frequent remains of long-past glaciers that dotted the area — so I had no trouble keeping my balance. And I had an unimpeded view of my granddad, who was now moving slowly, cautiously through the wheat field, shovel in his hand, blade down, handle up over his shoulder, as if he were holding a pike or some other weapon.

'It seemed like days that I stood on the top of the boulder. Probably it was less than an hour. And all of the time, granddad was prowling through the wheat field, as tense as I had ever seen him . . . or ever would see him.

'Then suddenly, without raising the shovel blade, as if he had been ready for action the entire time, he thrust.

'Just once.

'That was enough.'

Another pause.

All right, I suppose that Victoria did it for the dramatic effect; who could blame her? She had a rapt audience hanging on her every breath, and even if we already had an inkling — judging from the evidence in the pickup bed in front of us — of what was going to happen, we were caught up in her words.

I had to break the silence.

'What was it, Victoria? What did he kill?'

She smiled at me, almost as if thanking me for coming in with the proper question at the proper time. But she didn't answer directly.

'He leaned over and scooped something up with the blade, then, carrying the shovel as far up the handle as he could manage, he returned.

'On the blade was the head of a rattlesnake, its skull sliced nearly in half, with perhaps five or six inches of body extending behind the jaws. The severed end was crusted over with dirt and small bits of hay it had picked up as it had made its way through the field.

'Granddad didn't apologize for showing such a grisly thing to his little granddaughter. Quite the opposite.

''Sweetie, I want you to remember this, that's why it's important that you understand what I just did.'

'He rested the shovel — its curved blade still cradling the rattler's head — on the nearby stump of a tree that had fallen across the creek some years ago, and helped me down and away from the rock.

'He pointed a few feet away. There, still coiled as if ready to strike, was the body of the rattlesnake. It later measured over five feet long . . . without the head.'

'A big'un,' one of the men broke into the story to say. 'Though I've seen 'em six, seven feet long in good years.'

'Yes,' Victoria said, 'It was a big-un. It was rattling its warning to me but because of the sounds from the crick, and probably because of my excitement over the mouse-burial, I hadn't heard. Granddad saw it just seconds before it would have struck. He severed the neck just far enough beyond the head that the rattler was still able to maneuver into the undergrowth. He knew what that meant.'

'What?' I was a novice to rattlesnake-lore and had no idea what it meant.

'It meant, ma'am,' Tom Neilson said, receiving a nodded permission from

Victoria to continue the story, even though he had not been present back then, 'it meant that there was an angry, hurting rogue rattlesnake out there, one that still had enough of its vitals to keep on going for some time, for hours, maybe days, and that it no longer had the capability of warning anything or anyone that it was nearby. It meant that it was a real danger to any living thing in the area, pet, cattle, human.'

'You see, Lynn dear,' Victoria picked up the story without a hitch in the rhythm, 'Granddad's initial strike had left enough of the snake's body still attached to the head that the snake could live for quite a while. He knew that he was responsible for that — later, he apologized for missing the vital spots with his shovel, didn't know what had come over him, easy shot like that, he said. So he knew that he had to hunt the thing down, right then, and make sure it was dead. You don't leave an injured rattler free to strike again.

'I didn't realize at the time, or for years after, what an incredibly brave thing he had just done, scouring that wheat field for the rattler's head, depending on his eyes alone to find it.'

'I heard a story like that when I was a kid,' Neilson said. 'Man was changing a flat tire a few miles out of whatever town he lived in — this was back in the days of inner tubes rather than steel-belted radials. He wanted to be sure that whatever had punctured the tube wasn't still embedded in the tire, so he was feeling around on the inside of the tire for anything sharp.

'He found it. Pulled his hand right out of there and saw that what he thought must have been a long, sharp thorn had sliced into the meat of his thumb. He didn't think much of it. He finished putting the spare on the car, stowed the flat in the trunk, and headed on home.

'Halfway there, just as he got to the edge of town, he started feeling distinctly un-good, dizzy and sick to his stomach. Luckily for him, he was only a few blocks from his doctor's office. The doc took a look at his thumb, listened to his story, and called the state agent to request an immediate and emergency shipment of anti-venom.

'Man nearly died. Just because of a flat tire.'

I wasn't sure what to say. I had the feeling that, while Victoria's story might have been intended for all of us as an elliptical explanation for why she had been so adamant about being careful in moving the bales, Tom Neilson had told his story to *me*. I was sure his men had heard it before, and from the way Victoria was nodding, I was just as sure that she had heard it, also. Even Carver looked anything but surprised.

I was the only outsider.

In an odd way, I felt that through Tom's story, I had become a little bit less of an outsider and more of what might someday become a local.

'So this is what you wanted us to find, Miz Sears,' Deputy Wroten said.

'Yes. I had to be certain that it was here before I told you. And I had to be certain as well that no one touched the bales until we had a chance to examine them. The snake may be dead — I think that twitch was more a reflex than a living movement — but it could still have been deadly.'

'And if I had stacked it with the other bales and then broken it apart for the stock someday soon . . . ' Neilson said.

'It's possible it might have killed one of your cows as well. Or worse. The snake is dead, but the poison is not.'

Neilson removed his hat and wiped his brow with the back of his hand. 'That was quite a story, ma'am.'

'And one my granddad would be pleased to know that I never forgot. That was why, as soon as I saw poor Eric Johansson's body and heard Carver's explanation of what had happened yesterday, I began to wonder if perhaps snakebite rather than the consequences of a savage beating might have been what killed him.'

'But . . . ' I began.

'There'll be plenty of time for questions later, ma'am,' Wroten said, somehow just avoiding sounding brusque. 'Right now, I've got to get this bale and its . . . uh . . . contents back to town. Doc Anderson will want to see it when he gets home. All right with you if we leave it where it is for now, Tom? Can one of your boys drive it on into town? I'll radio ahead and let the boys at the station know it's coming and what they should do with it. And how *very carefully* they should handle it.'

'I'll drive it on in myself,' Neilson said.

'And maybe the rest of the men could check out the field. It would be helpful if we could find the remains of the snake. It must have been caught up in the blades of the combine and cut into pieces. I'd be grateful for as many of those pieces as you might be able to locate.'

The men nodded. They could do that.

'Then perhaps we should get going as well,' Victoria said, to Carver and me as well as to Wroten. 'I think that we still have several very important stops to make, and we might as well get on with it.'

15

The first stop was the Ellis place.

Deputy Wroten led the way again. He had checked in by radio with Deputy Allen to make sure that Eric Johansson's body had been picked up and safely delivered to the morgue in Fox Creek. It didn't seem like there was much reason to keep a watch on the Johansson place with the body gone and everyone who might be interested in poking around Eric's room safely in jail at the moment, so Wroten requested Allen to meet us at the Ellis farm.

He was standing outside the kitchen door as we made our way down the long driveway. He looked more than a little uncomfortable as the two cars pulled up side by side — the patrol car closest to the house, mine right up next to it. Perhaps Wroten had spoken to him at some point about the way he had behaved toward Carver that morning. At any rate, he had his service hat off and was working the brim with both hands as if he was particularly nervous about something.

Wroten didn't speak to him when he got out of the patrol car. He just sidled up next to the other deputy and waited, his face solid and solemn, looking rather like it had been recently carved out of a chunk of marble and had not yet been softened by wind or rain or erosion. His eyes were bright and hard.

This was Deputy Wroten in his *true* 'official' mode, not that John Wayne parody we had seen earlier.

I got out of my car first and went around to help Victoria, whose hip was, I think, giving her more trouble than she cared to let on, but before I could open the passenger door, Carver had slid across the back seat, exited the rear, and pulled her door open for her.

'Let me get this, Lynn,' he said. I was pleased that he had used neither 'Miz Hanson' nor the ubiquitous 'ma'am.'

He extended one hand and helped Victoria, although she did most of the

202

work herself. She seemed stiffer than usual, though.

I leaned over and whispered to her, 'Remind me to ask you how long you had planned on suckering Snake into decking you.'

She merely grinned at me and then addressed her attention to Carver.

'Lynn and I are going to wait here a moment, Carver. I do believe I shall need some help in getting to the house, so she is going to put her arm through mine and we are going to progress rather slowly from here over to where the two officers are standing.'

Carver looked confused, obviously wondering why she was saying this, particularly when it was readily apparent that she actually *didn't* need any help.

'You can go on ahead, dear, and wait for us at the house. I believe that Deputy Allen has something that he would like to say to you, and I think it would be better that he did so in relative privacy.'

Understanding flooded Carver's eyes, and he took off.

Victoria and I stood by the car door,

pretending not to watch as Allen took a step forward and spoke a few words to the younger man as soon as Carver was within earshot. I suppose that if we had listened intently we could have overheard the deputy's apology for manhandling Carver so atrociously earlier, but neither of us cared to do so.

To all appearances, we were examining a particularly lovely rose bush nearby.

When Allen extended his right hand and Carver unhesitatingly gripped it and shook it, Victoria and I made our way over to the house.

Wroten seemed satisfied with whatever Allen had said. His face was not quite so angular and stiff as it had been, although he was still solemn and unsmiling.

'Now comes the really hard part,' he said.

We knew what he was talking about.

We found Janet Ellis and Greta Johansson at the kitchen table. The room was bright and colorful, with a row of commemorative plates of varying sorts flashing highlights from a narrow shelf a foot or so below the ceiling. The window was open, its vivid curtains drawn fully open to let the sun stream in. The walls were a welcoming yellow, and the cabinets white, so the total effect was of openness and lightness and cheeriness.

The only mote of darkness in the room was Mrs. Johansson. She was still dressed in the worn chenille robe and formless scuffs. Her hair was still wispy and uncombed. But her eyes were more focused now and her cheeks held a little more color.

She and Janet were sharing a pot of tea. Her hand was wrapped around the china cup as if she treasured the warmth of the liquid inside, but it was steady and firm.

She looked up as we entered.

'Well, did you get them? Did you arrest those hooligans who murdered my grandson?' It was unsettling hearing the harsh words coming from such a fragile-looking woman. There was an undercurrent of hatred that seemed at odds with everything I had been told about her.

Wroten walked over to the table and settled himself into one of the chairs.

Victoria took the other one. Allen went on into the living room, apparently following instructions from Wroten, and Carver leaned against the sink not far away.

Wroten leaned across the table and placed his hand over Mrs. Johansson's.

'Well, ma'am. We arrested the men who beat your grandson. The ring leader made the mistake of taking a poke at Miz Sears here, in front of me and half a dozen other witnesses, so even though we don't have any direct evidence . . . yet' — he held up his other hand to forestall her obvious intention to interrupt — 'that he beat up your grandson, we will be able to hold him on an assault and battery charge until the coroner can complete the autopsy. Doc will know just what to look for. So I don't think the man will be seeing the free light of day for some time to come.'

Greta Johansson nodded her approval, but her forehead was still knitted and furrowed, and her eyes glinted with repressed anger.

'But they killed him, didn't they? They

talked him into doing whatever things they do out at that god-forsaken bar and then they killed him.'

Wroten glanced at Victoria as if asking for help.

Victoria responded, as I knew she would.

'Greta, dear, I know this is all very difficult for you. And I know that you think it might be easier if there is someone to blame. But the fact is that those men, however evil they might be, whatever evil things they persuaded Eric to do . . . they didn't kill him.'

'But . . . ' Greta was no longer angry. She simply needed Victoria to comfort her, to tell her the truth, whatever that might be.

'Eric was . . . well, he wasn't behaving the way that you would have wanted. He made some mistakes, serious mistakes, and because of one of them, those men beat him up, beat him badly. But he would have healed. And I would like to think that he would have learned from those mistakes and healed inside as well as outside, spiritually as well as physically.'

I wasn't so certain of that. From what little I had learned about Eric Johansson, I think that he would have remained a thorn in his grandmother's side for a long while yet. Some of my old friends from school had made the same mistakes, had begun the long, tortuous, and all too frequently one-way trip along that same road, and precious few of them had managed to turn their lives around.

I was by no means convinced that Eric would have been one of the few.

Truth to be told, part of me was glad that he was dead, for his grandmother's sake and for the sake of her memories of him. She would be able to construct — or maybe reconstruct — an idealized grandson in her mind and treasure him in ways she might not have been able to do with a living, breathing, wayward one. The one she would create would make no more mistakes. He would remain her darling grandson to the end of her days.

'Then how . . . ? What . . . ?' She needed to know more.

So Victoria, now holding both of her old friend's hands in her own very capable ones, told the true story, leaving out nothing.

Greta's eyes filled with tears.

'That was it? Snakebite? From a *dead* snake?' From the sound of her voice, she was blaming, not her grandson, but someone or something larger, more all-encompassing, something cosmic. I doubted that she would come right out and blame God — she didn't seem like the type — but she needed some way to keep Eric's death from seeming merely trivial, accidental.

'I'm afraid so.'

'But I've never heard of anything like that,' Greta said. I could hear her pleading for more.

'I have,' Victoria said. I wondered if she would re-tell the story she had shared with us earlier, but she didn't. 'And in a way, poor Eric was at least partially responsible.'

'Eric? How? How could he have known . . . ?'

'Of course he couldn't have known. That's not what I meant, dear.' She patted Greta's hands lightly. It made no difference, whether on the shoulder or on the folded hands, her 'There, there' gesture worked. Greta calmed noticeably.

'You see, Eric brought a number of ... bits of baggage, should we say? ... with him when he came up here to live with you. Partly, it was his attitude. Now don't try to explain it away, dear. You and I have talked often enough over the years that I could hear the pain in your voice when he ... well, when he didn't behave quite like the boy you had known and loved as he was growing up.

'Some of it was no doubt his grief at losing his parents so suddenly. Some of it was his desperate need to find himself, to build an identity that would protect him against any further loss. Some of it was a need to be independent, a need that struggled constantly with his need to have someone to comfort him and guide him.

'He had you, of course. But he chose to ignore you — don't deny it, dear, he did. And he chose instead to follow others, men who did not love him and did not care for him the way you did but who did not — in his eyes at least — threaten to smother him with love.'

'I never . . . I always . . . '

'I know. But he didn't. So he continued to play the role he had carved out for himself long before. There was his spiky hair, his piercings. Nothing wrong with them, of course, but they set him apart from others up here, made him more definitively a loner, an outsider.

'And there was his clothing.

'His spiky hair couldn't hurt him, other than perhaps to make him the object of attention. But his torn jeans could, and ultimately they helped to kill him.'

Greta had given up trying to interject or explain. She just sat there, listening to Victoria's calm, warm voice.

'You see, someone like Carver might be tempted to wear fashionably distressed jeans, say, if he were courting a certain kind of girl.'

Carver actually blushed at this.

'But he would know that when he was hiring himself out for field work, he would need to wear jeans designed, not for show, but for hard wear. He wouldn't wear jeans ripped across the knees, because he would know that he might have to get down on his knees to fix something underneath the frame of a truck, or boost something with his knee to get it to a needed height . . . for example, a bale of hay. He would know that the jeans were primarily for his protection.

'Eric might have known the same things. I'm sure Carver would have mentioned it the first time they worked together' — and Carver nodded slightly in affirmation — 'but he *chose* to ignore that. He *chose* to make a statement in the clothing he wore.

'And in the end, that was a mistake that he couldn't rectify.'

Greta seemed wordless.

I think part of her wanted to reject everything that Victoria had just said, wanted to believe that Eric had been absolutely blameless. But I also think that, deep within her heart and her mind, she was relieved. She had tried her best. She had given him the best home she knew how. She had tried to make him accept the responsibilities of becoming an adult.

And he had *chosen* to ignore her values and her life.

This time, Greta patted Victoria gently on the hand.

There was no need for a formal 'thank you' between two old friends. Her loss would pain her, perhaps for the rest of her life, but her loss would at least be bearable.

I knew how that felt.

16

The morgue in Fox Creek — as I discovered shortly thereafter — is nothing much. There's a reception area and an examination room, complete with a polished metal table and the requisite refrigeration equipment, adjoining the sheriff's substation and, conveniently enough, right across the street from Doc Anderson's office.

It doesn't get much business, but there are sufficient deaths-by-old-age, deaths-by-unavoidable-accidents, deaths-by-reckless-or-drunk-driving and so on to justify having it available when it is needed.

Today it was needed.

Death-by-snakebite-following-a-vicious-beating might not be a common occurrence, but there was Eric Johansson waiting on the table for us when we arrived, courtesy of one of the deputies from next door.

'Don't you need to check in on your prisoners before we do this?' I wasn't sure about the necessary protocols, never having been involved simultaneously in an investigation into a questionable death and several cases of aggravated assault and battery.

'Garton's the only one actually staying with us at the moment,' Wroten said. 'The others are on their way down-mountain for processing. We don't have the personnel or the accommodations to handle that many at one time. I'm not too interested in the others at the moment anyway.'

'Not inter . . . ' I think I started to sputter.

'Well, that's not quite the best way to put it I suppose,' Wroten said. 'What I meant is that Garton was the ringleader. I bet anything that if Doc Anderson can match the bruises on Johansson's chest and thighs to anything specific, it will be to the steel caps on a pair of boots that my men took off Garton before they locked him up and that are now in an evidence bag that will, I hope, keep them from stinking up the locked file drawer in my back room. The others are in some ways peripheral. Garton's the main suspect. And he's right where I want him.'

'Thanks to Victoria,' I added.

'Exactly, thanks to you, ma'am.'

'Well, Richard dear, we all have to do our part to keep the streets safe, don't we.' She smiled.

The three of us were about to see what could be discovered from Eric Johansson's mute corpse.

Carver had elected to remain at home with his mother and Mrs. Johansson.

'I've done enough,' he said when Wroten asked him if he would like to be in on the denouement. 'I don't think you need me there, and I know that I don't *want* to be there.'

So that left just us. The Three Musketeers.

As it were.

Inside the examination room, things got serious.

The body was laid out on the table in the center of the room, covered by a crisp, white sheet. Wroten peeled the sheet away from the head.

It looked, if anything, even worse than

it had that morning when we had first seen it. The bruises seemed too vivid to be real, the skin too white, the deep circles around the eyes too dark — they made it look as if his eyes were already beginning to deteriorate and shrivel back into the skull, although I was quite sure it was far too early for that.

The skin was icy to the touch. The body had been in the refrigeration unit most of the afternoon, although nothing else had been done to it. I could see by the edge of a T-shirt at the neck that it was still clothed as it had been when we found it.

'Would you give me a hand?' Wroten indicated where the sheet was hanging over the far side of the table.

I didn't want to. But then, I didn't want to make Victoria do it either, so I nodded.

We folded the sheet back until it lay neatly just below the feet.

Whoever had placed the body in the cooler had straightened the legs. The arms were tight alongside the ribcage. And there were no crusting patches of blood beneath the body. Otherwise it looked much the way it had — presumably — when Carver went in to wake Eric Johansson up early that morning.

'Now,' Wroten said. 'Can you take me through your thought processes? Show me what convinced you that Johansson had not been murdered?'

'Curiously enough,' Victoria said, 'I think the first thing was that I didn't *want* it to be a murder. As soon as I knew that Carver had found the body, I wanted to be certain that it wouldn't create difficulties for him. I *knew* that he could not have murdered anyone.'

'Exoneration by wishful thinking,' Wroten murmured. 'I'm going to have to remember that one.'

'Anyway, besides that, a number of things struck me. The first was the extent and the severity of the wounds and bruising. If some of those marks across the chest had proven to be relatively deep stab wounds, then perhaps enough internal damage might have been done to cause death.

'But since Eric . . . I suppose it would be easier, less personal now, to say, *the victim* had been conscious for some time — perhaps several hours — after the beating and had been at least partially responsive when Carver helped him into bed, that made it seem less likely that the beating had been fatal.'

'Come on now, Vic . . . Miz Sears.'

'Really, Richard dear, it's just us chickens now. *Victoria* is fine.'

'Well, you know as well as I do that beatings don't always kill right away. The victim might linger for hours, days, with severe internal injury and bleeding.'

'Of course, but that was just one of several things I noted this morning.

'Another was the condition of the right knee, at least as far as I could see.'

She reached out and pulled back the loose piece of material, revealing the battered, torn-up flesh.

'Notice that the knee itself is badly swollen and discolored. The scrapes and tears are mostly limited to this spot' — she pointed with a steady finger to an area that extended from an inch or so above the knee cap upward for another four or five inches. 'Here the flesh looks abraded, roughened. I suspect that if the victim were still alive, it would be oozing and bleeding.'

'Okay,' Wroten said. 'Garton and the others knocked him to his knees, then he tried to maneuver away from them, scraping his . . . ' He stopped suddenly and stared at the body.

'What's wrong?' I couldn't see what the problem was.

'What's wrong is that if Johansson had been trying to escape while on his knees, the damage would be on or below the kneecap, not *above* it.' Wroten tugged the lower edge of the torn jeans slightly, just enough to reveal that, sure enough, the skin there was abraded as well.

'Mrs. Hanson . . . '

'Lynn. That's good enough for me as well.'

'Lynn, then. I think there's a magnifying glass in that cabinet. Would you please hand it to me?'

There was. And I did.

He studied the area below the knee cap, then the area above.

When he handed the glass to Victoria,

he said, 'You're right. They're different.'

She examined the same spot, then handed the glass to me.

I wasn't sure I wanted to look that closely at the damaged tissue but I did.

It was mostly a conglomeration of reddish and purplish tissue set against the dead white flesh. But there was something more.

'Is that gravel?'

'Very good, Lynn dear. Yes, it is.'

'When Johansson was on his knees, bits of gravel embedded themselves into his flesh. It must have hurt like he . . . like Hades, but by that time I gather that he was too far gone and in too much pain elsewhere to notice it.'

'You are probably right. Lynn dear, now look at the area *above* the knee.'

I did.

The scrapes and abrasions looked slightly different, although I couldn't quite put my finger on what the difference was. But I could tell that there were no little grains of rock jammed into the flesh. There was, however, something else.

Something thin, almost translucent

under the bright examination lights, something that looked yellowish, organic, like . . .

'Broken bits of hay. Or straw. Whichever is the right word.'

'Actually, either word works. The thing is the same. Only the purpose differs,' Victoria said.

'Hay is for eating, straw is for sleeping,' Wroten added with a grin.

'But either way, you're right, Lynn dear. This wound has bits of hay — maybe we need words like *stray* or *haw*, except they've already been spoken for — ground into it. I couldn't quite tell for sure this morning, but with the magnifying glass, it is unmistakable.'

'Hence,' Wroten said, with the air of a particularly bright student asserting that, yes, two plus two does equal four, 'the victim had been boosting bales with this knee.'

'And not the other,' Victoria added. If it hadn't been her speaking, I would have said that she demonstrated the air of an even brighter student asserting that, beyond that, two plus two could equal seven hundred and eighty six, if looked at properly. 'Look.'

Wroten pulled the denim up where it was torn across the left knee. 'Good thing that fashion calls for symmetrical raggedness.'

He studied the exposed skin.

'Nothing. No scrapes, no abrasions, nothing.'

He pulled the denim flap down.

'But below the knee, the left leg looks like the right leg, scraped and torn. And I'd bet that if we checked, we'd find gravel bits there.'

He let the flap of denim fall. 'But we can leave that to Doc Anderson to discover. We're not interested in the beating. Just the ultimate cause of death.'

'All right, Victoria,' I said, holding up my hand and counting off on my fingers. 'First, you didn't want it to be murder. Second, he might not have been beaten severely enough to cause death, at least not within an hour or two. Three, he had been boosting hay bales with his right knee.

'I still don't see how that led you to snakebite.'

'Well, remember that Carver was certain that Eric had been drinking. He told us that the boy was hard to understand; that he was unsteady on his feet, wobbly, so much so that Carver had difficulty getting him up the stairs later; that he was breathing oddly in the car; that he had almost passed out by the time they got back to the Johansson place and was asleep as soon as Carver got him into bed — all of those are clear symptoms of inebriation. Usually.

'We also know now that Eric had vomited at least once.'

'Another indication that he was drunk,' Wroten added.

'Yes, normally. But several other markers were missing. There was none of the characteristic flushing about the face.'

'But the victim had been dead several hours by then, and there was the massive bruising on his head from the beating.' I could see the direction Victoria wanted to go but I couldn't follow her there yet.

'I'll grant that there might be some

ambiguity about the flushing. But when we examined the victim this morning, merely hours after he died in what would seem to be a state of extreme drunkenness, there was no reek of alcohol on his breath. None on his clothing. None anywhere in the room.'

'But . . . Oh, you're right. I didn't even think of that. Carver was so certain that I just assumed . . . '

'There, there,' Victoria said, patting my hand where it rested on the examination table, 'other than that you did very well today.'

'So that gives us point number four: all of the symptoms we ascribed to drunkenness could be attributed to snakebite. Everything pointed to his being drunk except one piece of evidence, which would have inevitably been present if he had been drinking.' Wroten was summing up this time.

Victoria: four. Skeptics: zero.

'Then at Land's End later this morning, Mr. Rafferty confirmed my suspicions when he noted that, in spite of behaving as if he were drunk, including nearly passing out and having problems concentrating, even when threatened by Garton with a beating, he had nothing to drink. If he was fired by Tom Neilson late in the afternoon and showed up at Land's End early in the evening, when did he have time to get that drunk, and where would he have done it? I'm quite certain that when you examine his car, which is still parked at the bar, is it not, you will find no evidence of a — what's the appropriate word here — a *bender*.'

'I've already checked out the car. I did it while you two ladies were sitting in the bar. One empty beer can in the back between the seats. Nothing more.'

'So he hadn't been drinking that night. Number five.' I held up all five fingers.

'Is that it, Victoria?' Wroten seemed satisfied with her conclusions thus far.

'It was enough for me to be fairly certain. And then, as we were driving back to Tom Neilson's farm, I made it a point to count the road kill.'

'The flat-frogs,' I said with a little giggle. 'And the mashed-mice. Oh, and the squished-shrews.'

Victoria stared at me.

'I made those up as we were driving. I thought they fit.'

'Yes,' she said smiling. 'The flat-frogs and the mashed-mice and the . . . uh, squished-shrews. There were more than usual for this time of year, which meant that there would probably be more predators than usual as well — and that means, unfortunately, that the probabilities of there being rattlesnakes in the Neilson fields was proportionally high. Shall we call it, corroborating evidence? Not enough to convict, but with the other five points, it certainly helped.'

'So all that remained,' Wroten said, 'was to find the snake. You have to admit, you were lucky with that one. If there hadn't been the accident with the truck, you would never have found it.'

'Not really. Eric reported feeling ill just after he had helped stack bales in the flatbed, so he took over as driver. No reason not to. He wouldn't be in traffic or anything like that, just driving down the rows of wheat. And that would mean that the other hands could help lift and stack the bales, and the job would be done that much more quickly.

'He couldn't have anticipated losing focus just long enough to drive into the nearby ditch. He had no idea that he been snake-bit. I'm positive that the pain from boosting all of those other bales against his naked skin would have been enough to overpower a tiny prick . . . and that is all that it would have taken.'

'Ahh, but the last . . . the *damning* piece of evidence. Where are the notorious fang marks, the two punctures, the vampire-like wounds that indicate rattle-snake?'

'There are not always two, Richard. Sometimes the strike is sufficiently off center for only one fang to pierce the flesh. But in this case, I think we will find something rather different'

She took up the magnifying glass again and, after adjusting the examination lamp, went over the wounded right leg carefully, inch by inch, until she said — unconsciously repeating Wroten, I hope — 'Ahh.'

She straightened and handed him the glass.

'Right there.'

He studied the spot she was indicating.

'Nope, don't see it. No puncture. Just one long scratch, like a stick or a thorn or . . . That's it, isn't it? That scratch.'

'I think so, Deputy Wroten. Doc Anderson will be able to tell for certain. But I think that a single fang hit the knee at an angle, tore a narrow, shallow scratch, and at the same time secreted enough poison that, since the wound was left untreated, the victim died.'

Wroten straightened.

'Care to look?'

'No,' I said. 'I'm more than willing to take your word for it, especially since the two of you agree, and *most especially*, since Victoria just called you 'Deputy Wroten' instead of 'Richard dear.' You must be back on track.'

There wasn't much left to do.

We covered the body with the sheet, straightening it as best we could to remove any wrinkles . . . the closest thing we could do at the moment to honoring the dead.

Anything more would have to wait for the funeral.

But at least we had accomplished several things.

We had demonstrated — to the satisfaction of the officer of the law in charge — the cause and circumstances of an otherwise suspicious if not mysterious death.

We had insured that a vicious hoodlum would be out of contact with the rest of humanity for a goodly time.

We had reassured a grieving grandmother that she had done everything she could have done to help her beloved grandson, a young man whom she no longer quite recognized and could no longer begin to understand.

We had upheld Victoria's confidence in another young man, whose name and reputation had already once been wrongfully associated with a sudden death.

And we had kept that young man, that fine, upstanding young man who was now my friend, from being charged with the death of Eric Johansson.

That just about settled the case.

Except for one lingering question.

'Tell me, Victoria,' Wroten said as we left the examination room, 'Just when did you decide *that* you were going to, and *how* you were going to, make certain that I would arrest Edward Garton at Land's End today?'

'Why, whatever do you mean, Richard dear?'

17

On the sidewalk outside the substation, Tom Neilson was waiting for Deputy Wroten.

'Bale's delivered. Two of your boys stored it in the shed out back. It's locked up. And they did it without getting bit. They did it *very carefully*.'

Wroten and Victoria laughed.

'Doc Anderson will have a look at it tomorrow. He'll probably do some scientific mumbo-jumbo and prove without a shadow of a doubt that the residue of venom in Johansson's blood and in the wound on his leg came from that very same sidewinder and no other.' Wroten was in a John-Wayne-testifying-before-a-jury-of-his-peers mode but no one cared. We were just glad that everything was settled.

Except, of course, that young Eric Johansson was dead.

Some things can be explained but never changed.

'Richard, dear,' Victoria said after a long moment in which we all wanted to laugh but none of us quite dared, 'would you mind driving me home? The Behemoth is in the shop and Lynn dear has been a wonder in traipsing all over the countryside with me, but I'm sure that she is tired of hearing my voice by now. Time to give her a break, I think.'

'Uh . . . sure, Miz Sears.' It was more than just us chickens now, so he was back to being a law officer.

'And I believe that there must be some paperwork you will need me to fill out. An affidavit or some such so that you can proceed with the charges against Mr. Snake.'

Oh, no. It was Helen Hayes again. What was she up to now?

Wroten looked slightly flummoxed but rose to the occasion like a gentleman.

'There's no need to rush, of course, but now would be fine if you have the time. I can get Sandy' — Sandy was the receptionist at the substation — 'to pull out the necessary papers.'

'Good to see you again, Mr. Tom

Neilson,' Victoria said, extending her hand to him. 'Hope to see you again soon. And give my very best to your mother.'

'Ma'am,' Neilson said, shaking her hand.

'And thank you, Lynn dear, for being so patient. I truly didn't have any idea when I called you this morning that I would keep you out and about so late.' She gave me a quick hug, then glanced rather ostentatiously at her watch. 'Why, it's nearly five o'clock. Almost dinner time. I am so sorry. But thanks again, Lynn dear.'

With that, she slipped her arm through Deputy Wroten's and steered him down the street toward the substation, already chattering to him about the details of her 'case.'

I stared.

She didn't just do what I was afraid she had done.

She *couldn't* have.

I felt my ears turning red.

Okay, she had done it all right.

The old . . . sweetie.

'Ma'am, Mrs. Hanson,' Tom Neilson said after a moment, drawing my attention away from the pair that was just disappearing into the substation.

'Please, it's Lynn. Only strangers call me Mrs. Hanson, and after sharing a . . . what was it, not a 'crime scene' but at least a place-of-the-cause-of-death scene, we are hardly strangers.'

'Okay, Lynn, then. It's been good meeting you. I'd heard a little about you being in town, and Victoria has told me a little about . . . your family. I'm sorry for your loss.'

He dropped his eyes to the ground.

Oh, 'Victoria dear', I'm going to figure out a way to get even with you for this.

'I enjoyed meeting you too, Mr . . . Tom. Even, or perhaps especially, under such unforgettable circumstances.'

There was a long silence.

Then Tom Neilson nattered on for a few minutes about nothing in particular, and I nattered back.

And then he invited me to dinner at the Timberline Place, the best restaurant we could boast of in Fox Creek.

And to my surprise, I accepted.

When I called Victoria later — much later — that evening to express my total and complete displeasure at what she had done, I also made certain to point out in no uncertain terms one more thing.

Dinner with Tom Neilson had been really quite lovely.

We do hope that you have enjoyed reading this large print book.

Did you know that all of our titles are available for purchase?

We publish a wide range of high quality large print books including:
Romances, Mysteries, Classics
General Fiction
Non Fiction and Westerns

Special interest titles available in large print are:
The Little Oxford Dictionary
Music Book, Song Book
Hymn Book, Service Book

Also available from us courtesy of Oxford University Press:
Young Readers' Dictionary
(large print edition)
Young Readers' Thesaurus
(large print edition)

For further information or a free brochure, please contact us at:
Ulverscroft Large Print Books Ltd.,
The Green, Bradgate Road, Anstey,
Leicester, LE7 7FU, England.
Tel: (00 44) **0116 236 4325**
Fax: (00 44) **0116 234 0205**

THE ANGEL

Gerald Verner

For months, Scotland Yard was interested in the mysterious Angela Kesson, who they dubbed 'the Angel', with her striking beauty. Her male acquaintances had dubious reputations. And in every instance, at the start of each relationship, their homes were burgled and money and valuables stolen. Though unemployed, she lived in an expensive flat, but there was insufficient proof for an arrest. However when her latest escort's home was burgled — he had been murdered, his head crushed like an eggshell . . .